Climbing Out

A Hawks Motorcycle Club Novel Book: 2

BY

LILA ROSE

Climbing Out Copyright © 2014 by Lila Rose

Climbing Out is a work of fiction. All names, characters, events and places found in this book are either from the author's imagination or used fictitiously. Any similarity to actual events, locations, organizations, or persons live or dead is entirely coincidental and not intended by the author.

Edited and proofread by: Hot Tree Editing.
Cover Design by: LM Creations
Cover Images: iStoke
Formatted by: Angel's Indie Formatting

ISBN: 978-0-9925170-0-7

Dedication

To my family, who has encouraged me to continue doing what I love.

Acknowledgments

I have found that this is always the hardest part in writing a novel, because there is always many who I want to acknowledge.

First and always Becky, Kayla and Justine. I'd honestly be lost without you three who have helped my work reach its fullest. Thank you.

Terri, Debbie and Dawn, thank you for your kind words and support.

Louisa at LM Creations. You are amazing!

Angel at Angel's Indie Formatting it was a true pleasure to work with you.

Ena at Enticing Journey Book Promotions. You are a superstar at what you do and I appreciate all your hard work.

Nicole, who Deanna is based off. I love and admire you. You're strong in many ways and you deserve the best in life.

My street team members, who have helped me pimp, support and begged me for more. You keep me going, knowing that you're all out there waiting to read whatever comes outta my head.

To the readers, I am so overwhelmed with the amount of people who came to me telling me how much they loved *Holding Out* and can't wait until *Climbing Out*. I only hope that you'll receive enjoyment out of reading this sequel like I have writing it for you all!

Deanna

As I watched Zara and her new husband twirl on the dance floor at their wedding reception, I wanted to throw up. Then again, I was also so fuckin' happy for her; maybe that was why I felt sick to my stomach…

She looked absolutely beautiful in her designer gown, even if her baby bump was showing. It was as though she pulled her dress from a page in a princess storybook and slapped it on herself. Bitch.

Only she deserved this happy day, and so many more after the hell she'd been through. Even though three months had passed, it still felt like yesterday when I'd come out of Griz's room at the compound to find Zara had been taken. The thought that I'd possibly lose my best friend shattered many things inside of me.

Yes, she pulled out of it, but I knew what something like that could cost you mentally. Sure, she seemed fine on the outside, but the inside would be a different matter. At least she had her boss-man to take care of her, and I knew he would.

Sighing, I sat back in my chair, and even though my insides were playing turmoil, I felt myself smile. Zara would soon be whipped away for her honeymoon in Fiji, the vacation they never got to have because everything turned into crazy-arse wedding planning mode. She was so excited about it, and when she got excited, other people also joined in on her thrill ride.

From the look in boss-man's eyes, I knew she'd be on her back in a matter of time. I chuckled to myself. There was no way I'd ever want to be in that situation. Okay, so yeah, I could do with the part of being on my back, just without the being married and knocked up bit.

My eyes searched out Griz. He stood on the other side of the dance floor, casually leaning against the bar; his eyes were on me. I squeezed my legs together. Goddamn did I want that man, but he kept fighting it, and right then I was glad he did.

My life for the next seven months or so was going to be

busy. I didn't need the distraction, and I knew as soon as I had my hands on Griz, I wouldn't ever want to let go.

I looked to my bag and saw the letter sticking out. I pushed it back in and zipped it up. That was the second letter; I got the first one when Zara's shit had started. Both were like a knife to my stomach. I thought I'd gotten rid of him from my life—obviously that wasn't the case.

I had eight months before he came looking for me.

I could only hope my plan would work.

If not...I'd be dead.

Chapter 1

Deanna

Four Months Later

Click, click, click. The sound of my fingers flying over the computer's keyboard was starting to annoy the fuck outta me. I turned up *Roachford* on my iPod sitting in its dock on my desk. My attention quickly went back to the monitor. *Buy, buy, and buy.* It was all I could think of.

Some thumps on my front door sounded over the music. I rolled my eyes, because I already knew who it was. Sighing, I put a halt on my online retail therapy and slid my chair back so I could bang my head against the desk. She was never going to get the fuckin' hint I wanted to be left alone for a while. I didn't want to taint her happiness with my...bitchiness.

"Open the flipping door, Deanna. I'm a woman on edge. I had a large slushy on the way over *and* I'm six months pregnant. Do you want me to pee on your doorstep for all your neighbors to see?" Zara yelled.

Fuck it.

I shouldn't have turned up the music, because now she knew I was definitely home, and *I* knew she wouldn't be ignored this time.

"Come on, cupcake; she's going to blow," Julian joined in on the yelling.

Scoffing, I got up and started for the front door of my two-story house. On the way, I took in the sight surrounding me. There was no way I could hide anything in the next two seconds, so I opened the door and prepared myself for hell.

"You." Zara glared as she cupped her hoo-ha with one hand while the other was pointing a finger at me. "We have some talking to do, wench, but move, 'cause I've gotta go." She pushed past me and ran for the bathroom that was down the hall off the lounge room, only her steps faltered before she reached the hall's doorway. "What the truck?" She gaped at everything around her.

"Incubator, we'll talk about how crazy our girl is after you pee," Julian said as he stepped through the front door and kissed me on my cheek.

I shut the front door and was geared up to knock myself out when Julian squealed behind me. I spun around and saw him clutching the *Ouran High School Host Club* DVD box set to his chest.

"Oh, my gawd! I-I've wanted this for years, but Mattie said if I got it he'd turn me out. Holy capoly, girlfriend, be prepared to have me living at your house just so I can watch this day-in and day-out." He sighed.

"Keep it," I said.

Julian eyed me suspiciously. He leisurely took me in from head to toe and then back again. "You look like shit."

I rolled my eyes and went back over to my desk, sat down and hit buy. A notice popped up on the screen announcing I was now the proud owner of a house in the Grampians.

Even though my eyes were still on the screen, I knew exactly when Zara had come back out. She stood behind me and slapped me on the back of the head.

"What the fuck?" I spun my computer chair around and glared up at her.

"What the duck, indeed," she hissed. "What is going on

here, Deanna? I haven't seen you in two, nearly three months, and this is what I find when I finally catch you at home?" She gestured to the room around her. "Are you starting your own Target store? What is with all this crap?"

All this crap was the only thing I hoped would keep...*him* from coming after his—well, what he thought was his—inheritance. If I spent nearly every penny, he'd have no reason to hunt me down.

However, I couldn't tell Zara any of that. She was in a happy place after having been through her own hell. I wouldn't bring her down again.

I shrugged. "Just doin' a little shoppin'."

She turned to Julian, who was still fawning over his DVDs. "Do you believe her lies?"

"Hen pecker, I believe her lies are so big I could roll them in a joint and be high off them for a year."

"See? We don't believe you." She pulled me outta my chair and studied my face. "Hun, please, please tell me what this is all about. And I mean everything—why you've been avoiding us, and why your house looks like a...a hoarder's place."

"Do you guys want a coffee?" I asked instead of answering. Though, making a quick escape to the kitchen didn't work; they followed me.

"Don't make me bring in the big guns to get you talking, Deanna Drake."

I laughed. "What, your mum?" I walked around the bench and readied the coffeemaker, and then turned to them as they sat at the kitchen counter.

"No—" she began.

I interrupted her. "Is that where Maya and Cody are?" I asked. Zara and Talon had won full custody for Cody two months ago, and they were ecstatic about it. So was Cody; he loved Zara, even more than his own mother. Though, no one could blame the kid; his mom was a slut.

"They're at school. Do you even know what day it is?"

"Sure, I was just fuckin' testing you, making sure you knew where your kids were, 'cause you know, once your tribe pops out of you, you're gonna have to be on your toes."

"Bullshit," Julian coughed into his hand. "Basic maneuver to change subject."

"That's the truth." Zara glared. "That's it; if you don't start talking, I'm calling." She grabbed her phone from her jeans pocket and opened it, fingers ready to dial.

"It's nothing you need to worry about, bitch."

"Five seconds, Deanna."

"Seriously?"

"Four seconds," she chimed.

"Who the fuck are you gonna call?" I snapped.

"The boss-man." She smiled.

"No," I gasped and shook my head.

"Yep. My hubby is already on speed dial. Four seconds, hun."

"Jesus, lamb chop, you're up to three seconds. Preggo brain strikes again," Julian said and sighed.

"If you call him, I will seriously be pissed at you," I informed her, and then leaned against the kitchen bench with my arms crossed over my chest.

"I'm willing to take your pissed-off mood if it gets me to the bottom of what's going on with you."

I closed my eyes and sighed. "Zara, please just leave it be."

"Oh, shit," Julian gasped, "she sounds serious, baby doll. S-she said please, and without cussing."

Zara nodded and said to me, "I know, but I can't let you deal with whatever you are on your own, Deanna. Friends don't do that. Also, if I recall correctly, it wasn't that long ago you were at my side through all my hell, and you wouldn't listen to me when I wanted it left well enough alone."

"Sing it, sister. Testify!" Julian yelled.

With a roll of my eyes, I said, "But look at how well all that turned out. And that was nearly a year ago."

"Tell me, Deanna," she pleaded.

I shook my head. "It's fine—nothing."

"Deanna!"

"Zara! Just let this blow over, and then everything will be back to normal." *I hope.*

"Let what blow over, buttercup?" Julian asked.

Shit!

"Nothin'. Look, I got crap to do, so both of you can just fuck off outta here."

Zara frowned, shook her head and then uttered, "One." She pressed her phone to her ear.

Fuck no!

I ran around the bench intending to tackle her for the phone, but she must have known that would have been my first move. She ran from the room.

"Hey, honey," I heard her say into the phone as I chased after her.

"Zara!" I yelled. "Don't you fuckin' dare." I glared as she stood on the other side of the couch.

"That's just Deanna in a bad mood."

"I will kill you," I hissed through clenched teeth.

"Why, you ask, is Deanna in a bad mood? Well, honey,

I'm not sure, but there is something wrong here, Talon. I'm worried."

Motherfucker.

I knew I had no chance now. If Zara was worried, Talon would try his best to squish that worry for her—in any way he could.

I was done for.

Shit. No I wasn't. I was Deanna Drake, and I didn't let anyone tell me what to do.

"Yeah," she said into the phone, "thanks, honey. I'll see you soon." She flipped the phone closed, and put it in her pocket while biting her bottom lip.

Yeah, she should be worried. I was going to do what any tough, don't-fuck-with-me woman would do.

I ran from the room, up the stairs and locked myself in my bedroom.

My door shook as it got pounded on. "Open the fuckin' door, Hell Mouth," Talon barked.

There was no way in hell I was opening my door. I was sure I could wait out the lot of them.

"Just leave," I groaned from where I lay on my bed with my arm over my eyes.

"You know I won't. You're worrying my woman, Hell Mouth. I can't let that happen. Not only fuckin' that, but who her people are, now are Hawks' people, and you're one of 'em. We help each other, and that means either come out here and tell me what in Christ's name is goin' on, or *I* come in there."

I snorted...and wiped away the stinkin' tears that broke free while I thanked fuck no one could see how his words had turned me into some stupid emotional woman.

But they had.

Because of Zara, I now had a family, one that was alive and willing to help. Jesus, I knew I had become a raging bitch when Zara wouldn't let anyone help with her problem, and now I was doing the same.

Ironic. Insert eye roll.

But this was different.

Now I totally understood why Zee was so damned determined to keep others safe from her crazy ex, because right then, I was willing to do the same. The only difference was that the wanker who would soon be after me wasn't an ex.

Fuckin' hell.

Was I being stupid with this act? Probably.

But I didn't want anyone to see the scared fucker I was

becoming underneath this facade. I thought I could take on everything.

I was wrong.

I was weak.

And I hated it. I hated myself.

David, Zee's weirdo ex, helped prove how much of a wuss I was.

It was a week after Zee's episode with him that Talon called me in the middle of the night askin' me if I wanted my payback, and if I did, I had to get my ass to Pyke's Creek.

What I thought I was prepared to do ended up being different than what I did do.

Griz

I was sitting opposite Talon in his office at the compound when his phone rang.

He looked at the screen and smiled. I knew straight away who it was before he answered it with, "Kitten, what's up?"

His smile fell from his face. "Who the fuck is yellin' in the background?" He waited for his answer, and then said, "Why is she spazzin' out?" He sighed. "You need me?" he asked, and then added, "I'm comin'."

He threw his phone to the desk and then must'a thought better of it; instead, he pocketed it as he stood.

"What's going on, brother?"

"Zara's at Hell Mouth's. Somethin's going on, so I'm headin' over there."

I also stood and asked, "Mind if I join you?"

He gave me a knowing smirk and chuckled. "Sure, Griz."

I ignored his reaction, followed him out of the compound and stalked across the graveled path to our Harleys.

"When are you gonna snap the fuck outta your shit and take what you want?" Talon asked as he placed his helmet on.

"Don't know what you're talking 'bout. There ain't nothin' I want." I sat astride my bike and belted up my helmet.

"Motherfuckin' bullshit. Wake the fuck up, brother. Hell Mouth won't be available forever."

"You of all people know I don't need another bitch to deal with." My bike roared to life.

"She'd be different," Talon yelled over the rumble of our bikes. "I think you know this, and that scares the fuck outta you more." With that, he kicked the stand up and took off.

Following him, my mind couldn't help but wonder off, thinking 'bout princess. Talon was right—she would be different, and that did scare the fuck outta me, because I've never felt the attraction I did for her for anyone else.

As if to prove the point, my dick hardened.

Christ, now wasn't the time to get a hard-on like some fuckin' little boy.

I got enough shit to deal with in my life than worrying 'bout her, but it had been too long since I'd seen her. For some reason, she'd been absent from everyone's lives for the last couple of months. I often heard Wildcat complaining about it.

There had to be an explanation. Anyone could see the love Deanna had for Wildcat, so for her to keep her distance like she had been, there had to be a huge fuckin' reason.

Maybe if I could find out what crap she was dealing with and fix it, then I could stop thinking about her and worrying every minute of the damn day.

And my shit won't stink either.

We pulled up to her two-story brick home in fuckin' suburbia. I bet her neighbours had their blinds twitching, searching and wondering why Deanna had two criminal-looking bikers walking up her drive.

Talon didn't bother knocking; he walked right in and I followed to find Wildcat and Julian sitting on a couch with a ton of shit surrounding them.

Talon let out a low whistle as I took in all the crap, from toasters to books to—was that a fuckin' vibrator sitting on top of the desk? I was afraid to look.

"What the fuck is all this shit?" I asked.

"That's what we want to know," Wildcat said. I glanced at her and could see the concern showing in her eyes.

"Where is she?" Talon asked as he made his way to his woman. He helped her from the couch and twisted her so she was in his arms.

"Once she knew you were coming, hunk, she took off to her room and locked herself in there," Julian explained.

I seriously wished he'd quit with the damn pet names.

Talon looked back at me and I nodded. We made our way down the hall—which was also full of shit—and up the stairs to her room. I didn't ask how Talon knew which room hers was, 'cause I sure as hell didn't know, and it kinda already pissed me off.

It had to be because Wildcat told him.

It had damned well better be!

Talon banged on her door and barked, "Open the fuckin' door, Hell Mouth."

"Just leave." We heard with a groan of annoyance.

Talon started to say something else, but I was too

occupied with my own thoughts to listen. What was going on with her? Why couldn't bitches just say whatever the hell was wrong with them, and then fix the fuckin' problem instead of doing this childlike shit?

After Talon's speech, silence met him from the other side. I was sure I heard a sob, but then thought, *that couldn't be right.*

But what if it was? I—we had to get in there to find out what was going down with her before she stressed the fuck outta us even more.

Talon turned back around and looked at Wildcat, who had followed us down the hall.

"See what I mean? Usually she'd be out here ranting and cussing like a sailor at us instead of this act," she said with a sad tone.

"She even said please before," Julian added, and Zara nodded in agreement.

Fuck. We all knew that word would never pass Deanna's lips unless it was serious.

"Do you reckon she'll let us have it if we break her door down?" Talon asked with a smile playing on his lips.

A shit-eating grin spread across my own.

"I don't think it'll be a good idea to poke Satan and test her," Julian said.

I chuckled. "I think it's fuckin' brilliant. Step back."

Chapter 3

Deanna

Eight Months Earlier

I'd made my way out to Pyke's Creek, to the destination where Talon had told me they'd be. I pulled my Mustang up, turned off the engine and then made my way behind an old, run-down boating house. The night was cold and misty; I wore jeans and a hooded jumper. I wasn't sure if this was killing clothes...what would one wear to kill someone in? I didn't know. I knew why they had chosen this area though. It was secluded. Nothing surrounded it except for bush land. The only road in was the one I just travelled. They could easily tell if someone was approaching.

Four large vans were parked there, and about ten bikers where standing around talking. Talon must have spotted me, because he appeared out of nowhere right in front of me.

"You ready?" he asked.

I thought I had been, so I nodded. Talon gestured to someone, and the back door to one of the vans opened. One of his men dragged the beaten form of David out and threw him to the dirt ground.

"You can't fucking do this to me!" David shouted.

"Bullshit," Blue laughed, "you fuck with Hawks, we fuck back harder."

Talon took my arm and pulled me over to the bikers now circling David.

"What's she doin' here?" Griz growled from the other side of David.

"She wanted her chance. I'm givin' it to her," Talon said.

Griz shook his head and hissed, "Jesus, Talon."

Talon just ignored him and called, "Pick."

My eyes widened as the bikers parted, and Pick shuffled forward. He looked tired, and seemed as though he was still in pain from getting shot. He was also showing signs of new bruising. I guess Talon hadn't been too happy with him after all. Though, no one could blame him.

"For the shit you caused, this is your payment. Do you accept?" Talon asked. "But realise this—if there are any blow-backs from killing this fucker, it'll all be on you."

Pick met Talon's hard gaze, and then stood taller and said, "I accept."

"He should fuckin' die like this piece-of-shit too," someone shouted.

Blue chuckled. "No one can touch him, or Wildcat will have Talon's balls for it."

Everyone laughed.

Pick winced. I bet he hated it was Zara and a couple of gay guys who saved his arse.

"All right. Let's do this so I can get home to m'woman," Talon ordered, and then turned to me. "Hell Mouth, you get first shot." He pulled a knife from the back of his jeans and held it out to me. "He stabbed Zara in the leg first, so I think it would be appropriate if we return what was done to her, to him."

I took the light-weight, agile fighting blade and smiled down at it. I felt pumped and excited for the fact Talon had let me be involved with this, even though Griz was obviously disgusted by it—I could tell from the scowl upon his handsome face.

Gazing from the knife down to David, my stomach churned.

"Hell Mouth?" Talon questioned, but my eyes stayed focused on David. He looked scared; his body trembled and sweat-beads showed on his forehead, but there was a cocky glare in his eyes. He smirked up at me.

Had he already known I was second-guessing myself?

"Just stick it in, sweetheart," someone said.

I wanted to.

I itched to.

But I was scared.

Me...scared.

Not something most would believe.

Though, they didn't know my past. They didn't know that every time I saw the colour red, I had to fight a panic attack.

And that was something I wasn't willing to do in front of Talon and his hot biker brothers.

I didn't know how long I stood there, staring at the knife and then at David. It wasn't until I felt warm arms circle my waist and heard in my ear a soft whisper of, "Darlin'," that it had been long enough for Griz to move around the circle to me.

To give me strength? I wasn't sure.

He took the knife from my hand, passed it back to Talon and then took my hand and dragged me from the group of leather-covered giants to my car.

That was when I heard Talon say Pick's name, followed by blood-curdling screams coming from David.

"Princess, look at me," Griz ordered, and when I didn't comply, he took my chin in his hand and forced my head up. "Get outta here and go home."

I shook my head, disappointed in myself. "I-I should have done it."

"No, you shouldn't have," he barked.

My eyes snapped to him and I sent a glare his way. "Yes, I should have. I'm a strong bitch, and I should have been able to gut the fucker, but..." I tried to pull away—to think—only Griz wouldn't have it.

He met my glare with an amused look on his heart-stopping, sexy face, which had been tanned by the sun and wind from riding that yummy Harley of his. "It just means, darlin', that you have a heart."

I gasped. "I do fuckin' not, you— you arse!" I took a step back from him and watched his large, calloused hand fall from my face.

Regret filled me. I liked his hand on me. I sure as hell

wanted more of Griz on me.

"I'm going. I have to go." I opened my car door and said over my shoulder, "You're a dick. You know that, right?"

"Sure, princess." He smiled a smile that made me want to drop to my knees and beg him to shove his dick in my mouth.

I shook my head and added, "No one fuckin' says a word, or...I don't fuckin' know. Maybe I'll send Julian upon you all for a year."

"Shit, no. No biker would ever want that to happen."

A surprised laugh escaped me as I watched him shudder. "Damn right," I said.

Gunshots echoed in the background, making me jump. I looked over toward the area where David was about to take his last breath, and I felt nothing but annoyance at myself for not doing what I so wanted to do.

"Get home, Hell Mouth," Griz uttered, which brought my attention back to his concerned eyes.

I grinned wide to show I wasn't bothered by what was happening just beyond the wooden shed.

"Don't tell me what to do, ya prick."

He burst out laughing, shook his head and walked off.

Present Time

Bang. I jumped from my bed to the other side of the room while holding a hand to my heart.

What the fuckin' hell? My door was kicked off its hinges, and the culprit stepped into my room.

"Griz, what the fuck?!" I yelled.

"Well, maybe next time you'll open your damned door," he growled.

What is he doing here anyway?

Talon, with a scary-ass-biker scowl across his face, walked around him, as did Julian and Zara.

"You made me do this. I had no other choice," Zara sighed dramatically.

"That's fuckin' it! I'm taking back the Harleys I bought for your little aliens," I said.

"Hang on a minute," Julian started, hands on his hip. "You bought her and Mr McSlap-my-arse's spawn Harleys and they aren't even born yet, and all I get are some DVDs? Let's talk about that." He stomped his foot.

"No," Talon barked, "let's talk about why in the fuck you're spendin' all your money."

Zara gasped and caught everyone's attention. She then

proceeded to slap her forehead and say, "I'm such a flipping idiot."

"I won't fuckin' argue," I offered. Talon sent dagger-eyes my way.

She looked at me with sadness in her eyes. "I get it now. I'm such a bad friend. Shoot, Deanna, I'm so sorry. Of course this is why."

"Zara," I warned.

No. No. No. I never thought she'd remember. She was as drunk as a skunk when I had told her. How in the hell could she remember?

"Kitten, you want to tell the rest of us?" Talon asked.

"Don't!" I hissed just as Griz's phone chimed.

"Fuck me, what now?" Julian sighed.

Chapter 4

Griz

I looked at the screen and my stomach turned. I wanted to put my fist through a wall. It was her again. This was becoming more frequent, but who was I to deny it?

"Gotta go?" Talon asked. He must have read my face.

"Yeah." I sighed. "Fuck!" I growled and looked up from my phone to meet Deanna's curious gaze. My brows furrowed and I turned to Talon. "You'll catch me up later?"

"Course, brother," he said with a chin lift.

"There will be nothing to catch up on," Deanna growled.

I scoffed. "Sure, princess." I walked to the doorway— where the door was now hanging from its hinges—and said over my shoulder, "See ya later."

And I meant it in every way, because I knew whatever was goin' down with Hell Mouth would be yet another situation where shit would happen.

She would need someone at her side.

Whether she liked it or not, that someone was me.

Shit.

And that was going to be more trouble I didn't need.

Guarding Hell Mouth's person was goin' to be a test all on its own.

I knocked on the front door, but there was no answer. That had never happened before, so one could say I was already on high alert. Kathy always had the door opened within seconds when I pulled up. She'd listen for my bike and be ready and waiting, eager to get the fuck outta here.

So where in the hell was she when it was only ten minutes ago that she'd rung?

I pounded on the door this time and yelled, "Kathy?"

Nothing.

Not one fuckin' sound.

That was when I heard it.

A faint cry.

I kicked my boot through the second door of the day and ran into the house.

The crying got louder as I got closer to the back of the messy house and into the bedroom.

"Fuck," I growled.

Stepping over Kathy's prone body on the floor, I picked up Swan, my two-year-old daughter, from her crib.

"It's okay, baby. Shh, everything gonna be fine," I cooed and murmured softly to her as I walked her out of the room, down the hall and into the dirty kitchen.

Fuck!

Was she dead?

She had to have been.

Jesus. Was the mother of my child laying on that floor dead?

In front of our baby?

Stupid fuckin' bitch. What in Christ's name had she done now?

Why the fuck did the house look like a bomb had hit it, and smelled like it as well?

I glanced around the kitchen, from the dirty floor to the bench tops, and some crap sticking outta the oven. The fridge door was open and empty.

Flipping open my phone, I looked down at Swan. She'd

calmed down enough to stare back up at me.

"It's gonna be okay, baby," I whispered.

Her little hands reached up and wrapped around the back of my neck. She buried her tiny head into my shoulder and sighed.

She knew.

She knew her daddy was here and was gonna make it all good for her.

Putting my phone to my ear, I rang Blue, because Talon had enough on his plate right then.

"Brother?" he answered.

"I found Kathy lying flat on her face in our kid's room."

"Be there with Stoke and Killer. We keepin' it low?"

"Nah, I gotta call the cops, man. People saw me walkin' in. But try and get here first."

"On it. I'm five or ten minutes out."

"See you soon."

I'd give him five minutes before I called the cops, and in that time, I left Swan in the lounge playing happily while I went to check what I already knew.

Kathy was dead. She must have passed after her call to me. I found her phone under Swan's stuffed animal-filled crib.

Quickly grabbing Swan some clean clothes and a new

nappy, because her other one was soaked through, I went back out to take care of my girl and called the police.

How long had Kathy been on the floor like that?

Shit, fuck! I could only hope that Swan never remembered what she saw when she was older. What type of blow-back could she have for seeing her mother lying dead on the floor? She was already not talkin', unlike most kids at that age who would have already tried to bleed your ears out with their constant babbling.

But my Swan stayed quiet.

I had asked Kathy to take her to the doctor's. She was forever telling me it was all okay, and that for some kids it took longer.

I'd bought that story for so long.

Now? Not so much. Something else was going down, and I was gonna get to the end of it.

After Swan was clean, I wrapped her in my arms and held her tightly. She liked that, always had, ever since she was born.

Christ. My heart was bleeding for her.

I should never have left her with that bitch, but all women seemed good at the start, until they'd try and control you. I wasn't having that, so I left, and then she'd told me she was pregnant. I was actually happy. Even though we weren't together, I thought it could still work. I thought even though Kathy was not meant for me, maybe she was meant to have a baby, to be a good mother in her own controlling ways.

I was wrong.

She never wanted Swan.

She still liked to party, and the few times I caught her trying to have a party in the same place my daughter was— let's just say things got ugly, and Talon ended up having to drag me away before I killed the bitch.

At least she wasn't dumb enough to cross Talon. Once he made an order, she followed through. The people were kicked out, and Swan was brought to my house for the night.

What I didn't understand was why she kept coming back for her. I'd told Kathy a million times over I'd keep Swan full-time. Only she wouldn't have it. Told me a man should never raise a girl on his own and that she needed her baby girl. She'd be lost without her.

Then, over the last ten months, things had gotten strange. Kathy would call and tell me to get my arse over to the house or she'd leave Swan on her own.

'Course I'd bolt over, and as soon as she'd heard the pipes of my Harley, the front door was opened and Kathy was disappearing into a cab. I'd take Swan to my house and tear Kathy a new asshole when she'd come to pick her up the next day, looking like shit.

But it was the same story every time—just that she needed a night out, needed to feel free, and we'd argue about letting me take Swan permanently. But of course, like the sucker I was, I gave in every time, because I'd never want my baby girl to grow up without a mother.

All that was about to change though.

And honestly, I couldn't be happier.

Fuck. I sounded like a dog for saying that shit, but I was. I was happy, because I knew Swan would now be in a tightly secure family. It was a family who took care of one another no matter what.

It was obvious something had gone down in the house last night, and the fuckin' knowledge my baby girl was here for it made me sick. Nothing like this would have ever happened at the compound, or even in the brotherhood. We party, but we don't it with the kids around. They were always safe at home with someone trustworthy to take care of them.

The front door opened, and in walked Blue, Stoke and Killer. They came over to the couch where I sat with Swan, who was now asleep in my arms. "Check the house, brothers. See what needs to be hidden, and what gives us clues on what went down. We've got about five minutes before the cops show."

"Done," came from Blue.

"On it," Stoke growled.

And Killer gave me a chin lift. He was the silent type. Didn't utter a word unless he felt it necessary, and he knew now was no time for talkin'.

They spread out and went on the hunt for me, while I sat back with my resting baby girl, thinking of the next step.

Deanna

Worry seeped into me. What was Griz involved in that had him running every time he got a phone call? It had to be something shitty, and if it was, no matter how much I wanted to tap his fine arse, I wouldn't.

Maybe just once? Get it outta my system?

No. I couldn't.

I looked up from the floor and into three sets of eyes that were all focused on me.

Fuck.

"Kitten, start talkin'," Talon growled and then shook his head. "Damn, but that shit sounds familiar. You two can't keep doin' this—keepin' things from me and my brothers so we can't help you."

"Hey," Zara snapped. "Don't go all angry-man at me. I only *just* remembered what all this is about."

"You can go angry-man on me anytime," Julian offered. I couldn't help but smirk; that fucker was always bringing a smile out of me when he'd say shit that would usually never be said, especially to an alpha male like Talon.

Zara turned to Julian and glared. He took a step back, hands held up in front of him and said, "I'm just saying. Whoa, momma bear, you are scary when preggo." He coughed into his hand. "Overprotective much?"

"Stop hitting on my man then," she grumbled. "Then I wouldn't feel the need to pee on him. It happens all the damn time. Whenever we go down the street, how do you think I feel when he's walking next to a waddling duck, while all the skanks' eyes are checking him out and thinking he could do soooo much better."

Fuckin' hell. She was on the verge of tears.

"Zara," I said, "get your hormones under control."

She stood straighter and said, "Right, yes. We're here about you."

Damn, I shouldn't have said anything.

"Kitten," Talon barked. We all looked at him to see he was tense, but his eyes were warmly focused on his wife. He took two steps and had her in his arms. "You don't have anything to worry about. I don't give a fuck if there are ten thousand women checkin' me out, and you shouldn't either, 'cause I fuckin' love the way you move, the way you look and the way you tell me off. No one will ever gain my attention for the rest of my life the way you have."

"Oh. My. Gawd," Julian whispered.

Something dropped onto my cheek. I looked to the ceiling to find what it had been, but nothing was there. It was then I realised my eyes had tears filling them, and one had escaped.

Fuck.

What was wrong with me? Why in hell was I leaking over shit like that?

I could only come to one conclusion—I must've been PMSing.

"Honey." I watched Zara melt into Talon. She whispered something into his ear that had him chuckling, and if I knew my girl like I knew I did, she was promising him something steamy in bed.

She turned in his arms back to me. "Now how about we all go to our house, hun? We'll have dinner, some drinks and we'll get all this sorted out."

"No, thanks. I'm all right here. You guys go ahead though." I walked around my bed and out of my bedroom, down the stairs and into the kitchen. I knew they were following me.

I stopped at the coffee pot and offered, "Anyone want one before you hit the road?"

"Hell Mouth," Talon hissed through clenched teeth. I turned to find him on the other side of the kitchen bench with Julian and Zara.

"Yes, boss-man?"

"If you don't get your arse in Zara's car, I will carry you outta your own house kicking and screamin'. What's it gonna be?"

"You know he'll do it. You've seen him do it to me," Zara added.

Sighing, I looked down at the floor pretending to think about it, but really, I just wanted to annoy him for butting into my shit.

Though, I couldn't really blame him. No, it was his wife I was gonna smother in her sleep.

Glancing up, I rolled my eyes. "Oh, all right."

Dinner at Zara and Talon's house was always something I enjoyed, no matter what kinda funk I was in. Honestly, who wouldn't? What I presumed would just be Talon, Zara,

Julian, Mattie and the kids, actually turned out to be all of them, plus Zara's parents with their foster daughter Josie, and Talon's sister Vi and her boyfriend Travis. Thankfully, Talon's house was huge enough to have us all there.

It was loud, messy and fun.

Until the front door opened, and in walked Blue and Killer. From just one look at their tense faces, Talon was outta his chair and in their little huddle at the front door.

"Oh, my. I'll never get over seeing so many delicious men in a room," Nancy, Zara's mum, said, causing Josie to giggle and Richard, Zara's dad, to sigh loudly.

"Mum," Zara snapped and made wide eyes, gesturing toward Cody and Maya.

"Oh, what? It's not like I said they were—"

"Nancy," Richard interrupted, "let's get these munchkins ready for bed." He stood from the table. "Josie, want to help, honey?"

Josie was still quiet around a large group, but if she was on her own, one-on-one, you could never shut her up—unless that someone was a male. She was still very timid around any man, even Mattie. Though Julian was girly enough, she never flinched any longer when he'd get near her. Still, there was one exception, and that was the youngest Hawks member, Billy Anders. Anyone could see the major crush Josie had on him. We could only hope he'd never be stupid enough to break her heart. But most of us were sure it was bound to happen, because he was such a womanizer.

Nancy, Richard and Josie disappeared with the kids from the kitchen and down the hall. They must have sensed something was going to go down, because in the next second, a piercing cry sounded at the door, bringing everyone's attention back to the group of delicious bikers.

Talon, Blue and Killer moved aside, and in walked—

Holy hell. It was Griz carrying a beautiful, little blonde girl in him arms who was screaming like a banshee.

What in the hell was going on?

I didn't know, but damn he looked good in jeans, biker boots, a white tee and his club's vest over the top. His eyes were a little more grey and hard, and his salt-and-pepper hair was a mess, but seeing it made me want to run my hands through it—just like every other time he walked into a room.

And honest to fuckin' God, he looked sexy as hell carrying that gorgeous little girl in his arms...even if she wasn't shutting up.

"Oh, my," Zara whispered.

"Zara," Talon called. She got up from the table and went straight into his waiting arms. He said something quietly to her and I watched—though I was sure it wasn't only me watching—as her eyes grew wide, her hand flew to her mouth and she nodded.

"New drama is a-blazing," Julian sang.

He was sure as fuck right.

Griz

Watching Zara being informed I not only had a kid, but that kid's mother had just died hurt me more than I thought it would—especially when she turned her eyes toward me, which were now filled with sympathy and pain.

But I didn't deserve it.

I hated the bitch who died, and right then, even though Swan was balling her eyes out, I was one fuckin' happy man. I had my girl—my baby—to myself, to raise in the way I wanted her to be, surrounded with people who cared about her more than anything, even more than their own life. That was what the brotherhood was about, and that brotherhood extended to their old ladies and rug-rats.

"Hey there, pretty girl," Wildcat cooed, capturing Swan's attention, who immediately settled a little. "Are you hungry?"

"She doesn't talk, Wildcat, but I'm sure she's hungry. Thanks, sweetheart."

Zara nodded, clapped her hands out to Swan and I was goddamn surprised when Swan reached out with her own small arms to be taken.

As Wildcat walked off with Swan, I watched them the whole way and was damn glad I did. Swan looked over Zara's shoulder and smiled. She smiled. My dead heart started to fill from that one little expression, only to skip a beat when my gaze landed on Deanna.

Fuck. She looked sexy. She sat at the table with Mattie, Julian, Vi and Travis, and while they all talked, her attention was only on me, and the look she was giving me—like she wanted to rip my clothes off—caused my dick to harden.

Shit.

"Griz, brother, wanna fill me in on what went down?" Talon asked.

"Like I already said, I found Kathy dead in her house. Swan was crying, so I broke in. I got the brothers to come first, and then the cops came and questioned us. It was obvious she'd OD'ed on something."

"Did they accuse you of anything?"

"They would have liked to, but a neighbour stated she'd had a crazy party last night, and that she saw me pull up not long before the cops did."

"Fuck, man." Talon sighed. He turned to Blue and Stack. "Did you find anything?"

Blue looked at me. I nodded, giving him the go ahead to talk. "Yeah, Talon, we found a member's vest...an old one."

"What the fuck do you mean?" Talon hissed.

"It was Maxwell's," I said.

Max was the one who left our club when Talon had taken over and cleaned the brotherhood up. Max still wanted to deal in hookers; he couldn't get enough of it. He loved the money they brought him, the attention and the pussy.

"We gonna have a chat with him?" Talon asked.

I ran a hand over my face. "Not tonight, man. I'm tired, and I want Swan to have my attention all night. I don't wanna leave her."

Talon nodded. "Fair enough. But tomorrow, we go talk with our old pal."

I smiled, because I sure as fuck had questions for

Maxwell, like why the fuck he would allow Kathy to have a party with my little girl in the house in the first place.

Jesus. The thought made me sick to my stomach. What in the hell had my baby seen last night?

"Calm down, brother," Talon ordered. "We'll find the answers."

Giving a chin lift, I turned my attention back to the table. Talon would have known how I was feeling, because he'd feel the exact same way if it had happened to his kids.

"What's the situation with Hell Mouth?" I asked.

"Don't fuckin' know yet. Everyone turned up for dinner and we didn't want to talk about shit in front of the kids, but whatever it is, she'll need protection."

I'd guessed as much.

"I need her keys," I said, while watching her at the table admiring Swan, who was sitting in Wildcat's lap eating some meat and vegetables.

Talon chuckled. "Kitten?" he called. Zara eyed her husband, handed Swan off to Vi and made her way over.

"Yes, honey?" she asked as she wrapped her arms around Talon's waist.

"Babe, I need you to get Hell Mouth's keys on the down low."

Her brows arched; she looked from her man to me, so I

supplied her with the reason why. "We're guessin' that whatever Deanna has to come clean about is serious enough to need protection. That right?" When Zara slowly nodded, I added, "So I'll have to move some things in, and if she knows before I get my shit to her place, she'll put up a huge fight. But if my stuff's already there..." I trailed off.

Zara smiled. "I'll get them."

Talon laughed. "That'a girl." He smacked her on the arse as she walked off.

"What about Swan?" Blue asked, his eyes shining with humour.

"I'll be taking her with me. Once Zara gets the keys, I'll need you two to go to my place and pack what you think I'll need from my room and Swan's—her bed and all. Then you'll need to go to Deanna's, fix her bedroom door if ya can and load all my shit in. If you can find fuckin' room."

"What you mean by that?" Killer asked.

"You'll see once you get there. You two okay with doin' that?"

"Pleasure." Killer grinned.

"Yeah, I just wish I could see Hell Mouth's face once she realises," Blue chuckled.

I couldn't wait to see it either.

Deanna

My stomach was in knots. Zara's parent had left with
Josie, and I knew the time was coming for me to talk.
Everyone was expecting it, and I knew if I didn't supply
them with the reason why I was going bat-shit crazy, Zara
would.

But something else was going down as well. I could
sense it. Zara was being cagey—one second she was with
us at the table helping Swan eat, the next she was with
Talon, and then next she'd disappear into the kitchen, only
to return and walk back over to the guys still huddled at the
door. Then Blue and Killer left, but not before staring at me
with...amusement in their eyes.

Yes, something else was happening, and I think that

something was at my expense.

Now, we were all sitting back at the kitchen table, with Griz joining us after he took Swan from Vi and sat her on his lap. The kids were in bed watching something on their TVs, and Zara had just come in from the kitchen once again—this time with Julian—and handed out coffees for everyone.

"All right, Hell Mouth," Talon began, and then took a sip of his coffee, "enough time has passed. Let's have this out."

"Looks like we came on the right night for dinner," Vi said, rubbing her hands together. I glared at her.

"Vi," Travis warned. He knew of our hate-hate relationship. Actually, I was sure everyone knew of it. It wasn't like I totally hated her—she had helped Zara in a huge way—but I hated the thought of anyone new stepping between what Zara and I had.

Was I jealous?

Fuck yeah.

Because I couldn't lose Zara. She was my rock.

"Yeah, well, feel free to fuckin' leave," I said.

"Deanna!" Zara snapped and looked to Swan.

I rolled my eyes and muttered, "Sorry."

"Let's just get this sorted so I can get my girl home,"

Griz growled.

Shit. My heart skipped over and stalled. That was something I'd wish Griz would say about me. 'Get my girl home.' Yes, fuckin' please.

Instead, I glared at Griz and asked, "Any chance you wanna fill us in on why the...*heck* none of us knew you had a kid?"

"No," he stated like there was never going to be an explanation, but I wasn't going for that.

"I knew," Vi said.

"Jesus." Travis sighed. "You can't help yourself," he said with a smile. "Precious, I think it's time we left."

"No way! I want to find out what's going on." She glared at him and crossed her arms over her chest.

"I'm sure you'll be filled in sooner or later, but it'll be less tense without us here, and anyway, we should get home to Izzy. The sitter can only stay for so long."

Violet actually growled. "You spoil all my fun."

"Thanks, man." Talon grinned.

"Yeah, thanks." I smirked.

"Hell Mouth," Griz said with a warning tone.

"So here it is, and I'm not going to repeat it, so listen—

beep—carefully," I said, once Travis had left with an annoyed Vi. Zara giggled at my attempt of adding in a swear word, but I had to add in something. It was killin' me not to, but when I looked at the sleeping form of Swan— Griz's flipping daughter—something in me wanted to behave like a grown-up.

I fuckin' hate doing this. I goddamn hate that I didn't know Griz had a kid when I want to be the one to have his babies...Holy shit, where in the hell did that come from? I want his kids? Fuck no! I'd be no good as a bloody mother.

"Sinner of all sins, how about you spit it out before hunter-man has a breakdown?" Julian suggested. I looked next to me at Griz, who had his jaw clenched and was glaring at me.

"Fine," I sighed. "I grew up in foster care, going through family after family until I came to the Drakes' house. They actually put up with my bad mouth and attitude enough, even going so far as to show me...love. Until, that was, their son came home from traveling. He didn't like me. I didn't like him. Jesus, do I really have to?" I whined the last part.

"Yes," Griz growled.

"Okay, okay. He came into my room one night and said

if I didn't put out for him, he'd kill his own parents."

"Fuck," Griz hissed, and then yelled, "Fuck, fuck, fuck!"

Swan stirred in his arms. Mattie jumped up from the table, and with tears in his eyes, he swept Swan out of Griz's hold and out of the room.

"I thought no swearin'?" I teased, trying to lighten the mood.

"Sweetheart, don't," Julian uttered.

Zara had tears in her eyes. Talon was as stiff as a board, and Griz...emitted a different kind of heat. His hands were clenched on his thighs like he was just waiting to hit something.

My heart sank and sputtered to life.

Fuck me.

They cared...and I couldn't handle that.

"Keep going, hun," Zara supported.

I nodded and stared down at the table. "I didn't know what to do, but I knew—I knew he was fucked up enough to do just that. And I would never want anything to happen to the Drakes, so I...I gave myself to him."

Shifting in my seat, I felt all their eyes on me and I didn't like it. I hated attention. "I let it go on for a year. Then I thought of a plan. So one night when he came into my room, I'd hidden a video camera. I told him no—like I had every other night—so he forced me. The next day, I thought I was the smart one and went to him, telling him to leave and stay to the fuck away or else I'd go to the cops and show them what he was doing. I-I should've fuckin' known. He went into a fit of rage, but then he left, so I thought I'd won."

I took a deep breath to steady myself. There was no way I was going to cry. I had cried enough.

"Mrs Drake overheard our conversation. She was devastated her son could do something like that. She wanted me to go to the police, but I didn't. I didn't want anyone to judge the Drakes for what their son, Jason, had done. Two months later, he broke into the house, and after he killed his father and tried to kill his mother, he came into my room—with blood all over him—to kill me too. Only Mrs Drake was still alive, and she called the cops. They came and he went to jail. Mrs Drake lived for another week on life support, and then passed away. It wasn't until I was at the reading of the wills that I found out—the day before their son had come home—they'd changed their wills and left everything to me."

I rubbed at my chest and then my eyes.

That had hurt.

It wasn't like I wanted to forget them, but if I let the memories get to me, I'd be crazy. I was nearing crazy when I met Zara three years later; she'd helped me and dragged me out of my darkness.

Julian's breath hitched, and I watched Zara wipe away her own tears while I waited for someone to say something.

It was Griz's hard voice that supplied a question to the silence. "How old were you when it started?"

"Sixteen."

"The fucker gets out soon, doesn't he?" Talon hissed through clenched teeth.

"Yes, and this is why I've gone a little crazy with shopping. I was hoping that he wouldn't come and look for me if he knew I've spent all his money—or the money he thinks is still owed to him."

"Are you sure he'll come looking for you?" Julian asked.

"Yeah. He sent me a letter about nine months ago."

"When all my stuff was happening?" Zara gasped. "Oh, God, Deanna. Why didn't you say anything? I'm such a bad friend." Talon pulled her out of her chair and into his lap.

"What did the letter say?" Griz asked.

"'Looking forward to catching up and my payment,'" I quoted. I witnessed Griz and Talon share a look. "What was that?" I asked. "What was that look about?" Because for some reason, I didn't think that look would mean good news.

"Nothing. Let's talk about this shit another time. Right now, I gotta get my girl home." He stood from the table and looked down at me. "I'll give you a lift."

I was sure I heard Zara giggle, but when I turned to her, she was straight-faced.

"That's okay; I'm sure Julian won't mind," I said, standing myself to stretch.

"Not at all, she-devil." Julian smiled, only it looked forced.

"NO!" Zara yelled. We all turned to her. "I mean, I need Julian here. I'm reeeally tired."

Julian's brow furrowed; I was sure he was thinking the same thing I was—how strange that sounded.

"Okay, weirdo." I shrugged. "I'll just grab my bag while you get Swan," I said to Griz, and with a chin lift, he left the room.

I bent over the table and whispered to Zara, "I don't know what you're playing at, but it ain't gonna work."

She smiled brightly and giggled. "We'll see."

Deanna

Swan slept all the way to my house in her car-seat in the back of Griz's Jeep Cherokee. As we pulled onto my street, I noticed two Harleys and one van parked out the front of my place.

"What's going on?" I asked, more to myself, but Griz answered with a shrug.

Stopping the car, I grabbed my bag and hopped out, and then leaned back in and said, "Thanks for the lift." Only Griz wasn't still in the driver's seat. He'd also gotten out and was now opening Swan's door to—I guess, get her out as well?

What the fuck?

"What are you doin'?" I asked as I slung my bag over

my shoulder, but before he got to answer, I heard the sound of feet stomping down my drive. I turned to find Blue.

"What are *you* doin'?" I asked with my hands on my hips and a glare in my eyes.

Blue chuckled. "Not much, Hell Mouth." He walked right up to me and handed me my keys.

Hell. What is going on?

"W-what? How? Why do you have my keys?" I screeched.

Blue looked over the car to Griz. I looked over the car to Griz too, who was now holding a tired-eyed child in his arms. The men communicated something through head nods and chin lifts, and that just pissed me off even more.

I turned to Blue, pulled back my leg and kicked him in the shin. "Why do you have my keys?"

"Fuck, Hell Mouth. Christ, why'd you do that?" he hissed as he bent over and rubbed his shin.

"No one is answering me or the main question I keep askin'!"

"They moved my stuff in, princess," Griz said.

My body froze. Had I heard him right?

Looking over my shoulder, I hissed through clenched teeth, "No way."

He grinned. The arse grinned, shifted Swan in his arms,

walked around the car, got close enough that our noses just touched and whispered, "Yes way."

Stepping back, I turned to shove a laughing Blue out of the way and stomped up my drive.

"Good luck, brother," I heard Blue say to Griz, "you're gonna need it."

Not wanting to hear his reply, I opened my front door just as Killer and Stoke were coming out. Upon one look at my face, they both smiled widely and moved out of my way.

"Have a nice night, Hell Mouth." Stoke laughed as I picked up a cushion and threw it at him. They walked out the front door and closed it behind Griz.

Oh, my fuckin' God. Was Griz really staying here?

My heart took off outta control regarding a certain thought of seeing Griz every night and morning, walking around my house in nothing but his boxers.

My hoo-ha sang for joy.

I had to have proof.

Dropping my bag to the couch, I made my way down the hall and up the stairs. I opened the door to the first spare room. What was full of shit this morning, now held a kid's bed with some side cushion-thingy on it. I guess that was to stop Swan from falling out.

Wait a goddamn minute!

Swan was stayin' here as well?

Oh, shit.

Fuck.

I couldn't have a kid around. It'd learn bad shit from me. What was he thinkin'?

"I see you found Swan's room," Griz said from behind me, causing me to jump.

"Jesus, a warning is nice before you sneak up on someone." I looked to Swan in Griz's arms; she seemed so tired, with her blue eyes blinking up at me and her head resting against Griz's chest.

I wondered if he'd let my head rest on his chest too?

Shaking my head, I looked up to a smiling Griz. What the fuck was he smiling about?

"Look, you can't do this. You can't just move yourself and *your daughter* in here. This isn't going to work." I shook my head.

"Its fine and it's staying this way until your shit is over," he said in his don't-give-me-any-bullshit voice.

"You wanna risk your daughter?" I asked.

"She won't be at risk. During the days while I'm busy, she'll be with Wildcat until I can get a sitter or organise some childcare. Then at night—well, I'll be here, so no risk will come to her...or you."

Why was my heart beating like the *Jaws* soundtrack?

Because this was going to either kill me or—yeah, let's not go there, because that thought was even scarier.

I was sure Griz was shocked that I didn't argue with him. I muttered a final "whatever" and left the room. There was no point anyway, not when he held an exhausted Swan in his arms. Plus, there was always tomorrow. For now, I'd let him have his way and crash in my spare room.

Though, as I changed into my cami and boy shorts for bed, my mind wouldn't stop wandering from the thought of Griz sleeping in my house—sleeping not far from me.

What is he dressed in?

How far is the sheet pulled up over him?

Does he have a sheet on at all?

Should I check if he even has a sheet on?

Fuck! This was really playing with my mind.

There was only one thing for it. I rolled over on my side, opened the bedside table and pulled out Vinny.

Vinny the Vibrator had many times entertained me enough to forget whatever else was going on around me. I could only hope he would fulfil his job tonight, or else Griz may just call the cops and accuse *me* of rape.

Pulling the sheet back over me, I quickly wiggled out of my shorts and was just about to go to town…when I heard my bedroom door open.

"What are you doing?" I yelled at Griz.

"Goin' to sleep, darlin'. I'm buggered."

He took off his vest and pulled his tee over his head, showing me he was ripped and tattooed galore over his pecs and upper arms.

Frozen in my state of admiration, and thankin' myself for leaving the curtains open enough, I could clearly see him unbutton his jeans and tug them off, leaving him in black boxers. He pulled the sheet down a bit and hopped into the bed next to me, lying on his back.

"Um—"

"Don't start, sweetheart; let's just sleep."

"But—"

"Darlin', I don't want to fight."

"Why aren't you in the room with your daughter?" I asked, and yes, still with Vinny waiting patiently at my entrance.

"I don't know if you noticed, but there was only her bed in there."

"I have other spare rooms."

"Yeah, with that much shit in there, no one could fuckin' breathe."

"Griz, I really don't think this is a good idea," I stated, even though I was ready to throw Vinny away, jump onto Griz's rhythm stick and go for a ride.

"Too bad, darlin', 'cause I ain't movin'."

He rolled onto his side so his back was toward me. What in the hell was I supposed to do now? I had a hot male—who was tired and seemed in a mood—sleeping next to me, while I lay with my legs apart and my vibrator ready for the green go-sign.

Decisions, decisions.

Can I continue in what I so want and need? Or should I do the proper thing and put Vinny away for another night.

To hell with it.

My hoo-ha yelled in victory.

Flippin' the switch, Vinny buzzed to life, and with one thrust forward I moaned as he slipped into my willing, wet pussy.

"What the fuck?!" Griz yelled. It was in seconds, I was sure, that he'd flipped over to face me, went up on his giant, muscular, tattooed arm and threw the covers back with his other hand. "W-what?" He looked down at Vinny, and then up at me with a look of lust, anger and desire all in one.

67

"Well, you fuckin' came in at the wrong time, and there is no way I'm willing to stop," I supplied.

In my little rant, my hand moved Vinny and a groan left my lips. I arched off the bed and settled down, only to open my eyes to meet the hooded grey stare of Griz.

"Fuck," he hissed.

In yet another second, he was off the bed and over in the corner of the room.

"Y-you can't do that shit while I'm in here." He glared and then looked away to the floor.

"Bullshit. It's my room; you came in here, so suffer the consequence." I giggled, but it quickly turned into a moan as Vinny hit just the right spot.

"Jesus!" Griz groaned.

I found that I was turned on even more than usual having Griz in the room and watching me with hungry, but pained eyes. I pulled Vinny out, only to push him back in swiftly, and hissed when he reached that wonderful spot inside of me again.

I opened my eyes as I pulled Vinny out and laid him against my clit. My breath hitched; I knew I was close.

It was the fastest I would ever been able to make myself come in my whole life.

But I wasn't ready quite yet.

I needed to play with Griz a little more.

Moving Vinny away, I looked over at Griz, who was still standing in the corner with a tent in his boxers watching me. "You could come and join me?" I whispered to the quiet room.

He shook his head. "W-we can't do this, princess."

I pouted. "And why the fuck not? It's obvious you want me, and I've been forward enough to let you know I'd do you. So what's stopping you?"

"My child in the other room," he growled.

Pulling the sheet over me, I shook my head and said, "No, I don't think that's it. 'Rents have sex all the time with their children in the house. It's something else, but what?"

"You're too young," he said.

I scoffed, "Get over it." Throwing the sheet back off me, I grabbed Vinny tightly and plunged him into my still-wet pussy. A moan filled my mouth as I grabbed my breast and arched. "Oh, God, Griz. You better hurry before I come."

"Shit," he uttered and then cleared his throat. "Darlin', you better fuckin' stop."

"Hell, Griz. I can't. It feels so good, babe." Vinny and I were having the time of our lives as he slid back and forth into my moist tunnel.

"Fuck, darlin'. Fuck." Griz groaned. "Two can play at this," he growled quietly.

Looking back over at him, my eyes widened as I watched him pull the front of his boxers down and palm his large, hard erection, and then proceeded to masturbate.

Holy shit!

Griz

I could not fuckin' believe what I was doing—standing over in the corner of the room with my dick in my hand—and as I tugged it, I watched with pure voyeuristic desire as Deanna's pussy engulfed her vibrator laying in her bed where I was just beside her.

Actually, that was what she *had* been doing…until I took my cock in my hand.

Now, her greedy eyes were trained on me and my body, and her vibrator was set aside.

She rubbed her legs together, got up on her elbows and licked her lips.

A groan fell from mine. I wanted more that any-fuckin'-

thing to take a leap and have my dick buried inside of her willing snatch.

But I didn't.

Why?

Many reasons, but the main one was that once I was in her, I wouldn't want to leave.

Ever.

That was a fuckin' scary thought.

Shit. I was so close to coming just from watching her watch me. I needed to stop, or at least slow the fuck down so I didn't embarrass myself and come too quickly.

"Griz," she moaned, "please."

Jesus Christ!

"Call me by my name, darlin'."

Her eyebrows rose. She didn't understand what I was askin'. Instead, she said, "Griz."

I shook my head and slowed my hand down even more. "No, princess. My real name."

I bet she didn't even know it, and the thought of that fuckin' hurt. Why in the hell would she want to screw someone whose name she didn't even know?

I watched her face light up and she licked her lips. She ran her hand over her breasts, down her stomach and finally spread her legs, dipping her fingers into her juices. "Please come and fuck me...Grady."

Motherfucker.

With a growl, my boxers hit the floor and I was on the bed in seconds, hovering over her on all fours.

A smile spread across my face as I watched her lay back and laugh.

"You should have told me that's all I needed to do, and I would have uttered your name a long fuckin' time ago." She grinned.

I brought my face closer to hers and hissed, "Say it again."

She licked her lips and whispered, "Grady." Only to end with a moan as my fingers slipped into her wet core.

"Fuck, darlin', you're so wet for me," I growled.

She panted, "Only for you." It was then she reached up, wrapped her arms around my neck and pulled me down to her. Our lips collided in an urgent frenzy, and then our tongues entwined together while my fingers fucked her.

Pulling away was one of the hardest things I've ever had to do, but I wanted something else even more. Plus, I needed oxygen, because right then, it seemed my body wasn't getting enough.

"Jesus, Dee," I growled as my chest rose and fell in a rapid speed. At least mine wasn't the only one. I watched as

Deanna's perky breasts rose and fell just as quickly. "I need to taste you." That statement was a rumble from my chest. "Fuck, I need it more than air right now. Will you let me?"

"What're you askin' for, babe?"

"Some women don't like it." *Where I loved to give it.*

She ran her hand over my cheek and grinned. "Grady." *Hell, I loved hearin' my name on her lips.* "I want you to taste me. My pussy needs the attention of your mouth. Can you do that for me?"

With wide eyes, I hissed, "Christ." Giving her a quick, hard kiss, I moved down her body and spread her legs to accommodate my large frame as I laid my body down. I pulled her ass up with my hands and dove my face into her snatch. Even if my dick was beggin' to be where my mouth was lickin', bitin' and suckin', there was no way I was gonna miss out on the chance to taste her sweet juices. Because I knew once my cock got his way, we'd probably be over in a matter of seconds.

Dee's hands slid into my hair and held me tightly to her, but she needn't have worried—there was no way I was goin' anywhere until I felt her come on my tongue.

She moaned, hissed and swore as my lips, tongue and teeth drove her crazy.

To watch her beautiful body arch as she yelled my

name was something else. And it was something I would never get enough of. She was sexy—a real, hot piece of work.

Fuck.

I was in trouble.

"Grady, damn, Grady, I'm gonna come," she moaned.

Jesus, I was pretty sure I was gonna come myself. What didn't help was that I was thrusting my cock into the bed, and the friction of it, as well as watchin' and tasting her, wasn't doing me any good. I was seconds away.

"Do you wanna come on my tongue or my fingers?"

"Hell...oh, God. Um, fingers. I want your fingers. Is that okay?"

"As long as I get to clean it all up with my mouth, it's fuckin' fine with me, darlin'." I pulled my face back and inserted my fingers back into her tight pussy. She groaned loud and sweet as my fingers drove back and forth and my thumb rubbed at her clit.

"Grady, fuck. Faster, babe. Oh, hell."

Shit, she was so damn hot.

Her eyes met mine and that was my undoing. As she came all over my fingers, I pumped my hips into the bed and blew my load all over the sheets, causing both of us to cry out. After she'd come down, I removed my fingers, and she watched me and whimpered as I licked them clean and then bent my head to clean away all her come with my mouth and tongue.

I got up on all fours, and made my way back up so I was over her where we'd started.

"Now it's your turn." She grinned.

I felt my cheeks heat and I knew she'd seen them, because her eyes widened a fraction. "Too late, darlin'. Watching you and your hot body move under my face and fingers had me shoot my load onto the bed like some fuckin' eager teenager."

Her mouth opened in shock. She threw her hand over her mouth to cover the giggle that escape, but it was too late; I'd heard it.

"You laughin' at me, woman?" I mock-growled. She nodded and rolled to her side, though she shouldn't have, because now I had the chance to smack her arse good and hard.

She stopped laughin' straight away and ended up moaning. "Fuck me. My darlin' likes rough play," I groaned.

She looked up at me with pleading eyes. "Wanna try again, Mr Teenager?"

I rolled to the side and pulled her close. She rested her

head on my chest. "Jesus. You're gonna kill my old body."

"Don't say that."

She sounded so serious I brought her head up with my hand under her chin to see the look on her face. She had said it with a sombre expression.

"Darlin'?"

"Please...fuck. Just don't say shit like that. I-I can't have you dying on me too."

Stupid fuckin' dick—that's what I was.

"Sorry, sweetheart."

"Great." she hit my chest. "Now I've put a downer on what was the best head-job in my whole life."

I grabbed her hand and said, "No, you haven't. And seriously, best?"

"Well, let's not get ahead of ourselves. There still could be better out there."

I rolled her on top of me so she lay flat along my body. My dick went straight to attention, but I wasn't gonna start anything again tonight. We needed to take this slow.

Instead, I smacked her arse again and growled at her lips, "You have been good and fucked by my mouth and fingers, darlin'. No one, and I fuckin' mean no one, is gonna have a chance to do the same while I'm in the picture." I squeezed her arse in my hands. Her eyes widened. "You get that, darlin'? No one. Because I plan to stick around for a long fuckin' time. Now that I've tasted you, I want nothing else."

"Even if this scares you?" she uttered.

It was my turn for my eyes to widen.

How in the fuck had she known?

She sighed and laid her head on my chest. "It scares me too, Grady," she whispered.

Well damn.

Chapter 10

Deanna

Stretching in the morning after a good and proper tongue lashing felt great. I reached over to the side Griz...Grady occupied last night with a smile on my lips, only to find it empty.

It was then I heard voices and the TV coming from downstairs, because my bedroom door was open. I realised then that Blue, Stoke and Killer must have fixed my bedroom door, as well as moving Grady and Swan in last night. That was nice of them.

Oh, hell, when did I ever fuckin' think nice things? It was happenin' already. I was—and felt—less bitchy. I wondered what would happen to me if I truly got fucked by Grady.

A laugh escaped me. I couldn't wait to find out.

After stretching again, I then ripped the sheet from my naked body and got out of bed. I headed straight for my ensuite and started the shower.

Though, maybe I shouldn't have had a shower first.

Maybe I should have gone downstairs to see Grady instead, because now, as I washed my blonde hair, I had more time to second guess...everything.

What would happen if things had changed for him? What if he didn't really mean what he said last night? *No, it wasn't a dream. He had said he wanted something to start between us.*

But then, what happens if this—us—did start...seeing each other? There was Swan to consider in this. It wouldn't be just a relationship with Grady, but his daughter as well.

I wasn't good enough to be around her.

Was I even good enough for *him*?

Fuck. Now I felt like shit, and mean. Maybe I shouldn't have started anything last night.

Crap. I just didn't know.

There was only one way to decide—go down and face the music. I'd learn how he would be with me and see if he wanted me around his daughter.

I turned off the water and got out of the shower. After

quickly drying myself, I dressed in black slacks and a white shirt; I had to get to work at the library in two hours. With wet hair hanging loose and bare feet, I made my way downstairs.

Walking into the lounge, I found Swan sitting on the carpeted floor playing with two dolls and some blocks, while some cartoon played on the TV.

What was I supposed to do, keep walkin' or talk to her? *I need to grow some balls.* So I walked over to her and sat down beside her.

"Morning, Swan."

She looked up at me and smiled shyly, and then went back to her toys.

"Do you wanna build something with me?"

She shook her head and pointed to something on the other side of her—books. I reached over and picked one up. "Do you want me to read this to you?"

She nodded. I could do that. I read *Spot Bakes a Cake,* and then we moved on to another Spot adventure. But when I started *Whose Nose,* that was when Swan moved to sit on my lap, and my heart constricted when she rested her head against my chest.

After her last three books—all *Hairy Maclary* ones, which I loved—she looked up at me, smiled and uttered in such a soft sweet voice, "Ta."

I helped her hop off my lap and back onto the floor, and then said, "I love reading, Swan. So maybe later, when I get back home from work, we can read some more?" She beamed up at me; I guess that was my answer.

Standing up, I turned to go and find Grady, only to see him standing in the kitchen-lounge doorway, leaning against it with his arms crossed over his black-teed chest.

Fuck, he was hot.

With a chin lift, he turned and walked back into the kitchen. I followed.

He was on the other side of the island bench, and once I walked in and over to stand on the opposite side, he said, "I was gonna come wake you. I'm glad I didn't have to...because what I saw in there—you with my daughter, reading to her—means more to me than you'll ever know."

"Um."

"Get your arse around here," he ordered on a growl.

I got around there, and when I did, he pulled me against him and attacked my mouth like a starved man. I wrapped my arms around his neck and went on my tippy-toes to show him what he just said meant more to me than *he* would ever know.

He pulled away and looked down at me. "Fuck. You

look hot, darlin', looking all professional."

I grinned up at him and said, "You look hot yourself, biker-man. So hot, I'm wet already."

He closed his eyes and groaned. "Shit, Dee. I want my fingers in you so much right now, just so I can taste you again."

"It'll have to be later, babe. Now that Swan's awake, we have to be careful."

He tilted his head back and let out a roar of laughter. I hit his chest. I didn't know what in the fuck he was laughing at, but I knew it was at my expense.

I tried to move out of his embrace, but he held strong, and after he'd calmed enough, he looked down at me with amused eyes. Though, they also held a sweet heat that had my hoo-ha convulsing.

"Darlin', you saying that, wanting to protect my daughter makes me fuckin' happy." He grinned. "Makes me realise I was being a stupid dick being worried about our age difference. But most of all, what you just said turned me the hell on, and now I've got to have a taste before I take Swan over to Wildcat's." With that, I found his hand down my pants and in my underwear. I gasped at the abruptness, and then whimpered when his eyes took on a wicked gleam as his fingers ran along my folds and then inserted into my already wet pussy.

"Hell, darlin', I wish I had time to wet my dick with this," he pumped his fingers in and out, causing me to moan, "with your sweet pussy, but I don't, so this will have to hold me off." He removed his fingers, and my eyes grew as I watched him raise his hand to his mouth to lick and suck my juices off. A growl escaped his chest. He closed his eyes in what looked like ecstasy.

"Jesus, Grady," I hissed and whimpered. I was so turned on I needed a release, or I'd be one cranky bitch all day. "Please tell me you have time to fuck me. Tell me you'll go drop Swan off now, come back here and fuck me hard and good."

He smiled down at me and shook his head. "Sorry, princess, I've got shit I have to do, but at least I know you'll be ready for me tonight." He stepped back, slapped my arse and walked out of the room chuckling.

"You leave me like this and you won't see anything tonight," I yelled to him.

"Yeah, right, we'll see," he yelled back.

Yes, we would see.

Griz

Fuck, it was so hard to walk out the door with Swan and not go back to screw my woman like she wanted. Hell— like *I* wanted. But as I said, I had shit to do, so after dropping off Swan at Wildcat's, I headed to the compound. Upon walking through the front door, down the hall and into Talon's office, I knew he knew I'd be coming, because not only was Talon there, but Blue, Killer, Stoke and Pick were there also.

"I guess you already know what I want," I said.

"I do, brother, 'cause I'd want the same goddamn thing." Talon nodded. "The brothers here all agree; we're going with you in case it gets ugly."

I looked to the group of men around me, fuckin' proud and happy I had these men, these brothers, in my life. "All right, let's do this. Let's go see our old member for some answers."

We all loaded onto our Harleys and left the compound to head across Ballarat to Lal Lal, where we knew Maxwell resided. He lived on a dead-end street, but a street that was busy with houses and families. Though, no matter where he lived and who saw us approaching, I still had to find the truth, and he'd better fuckin' give it to me, or he'd soon be a dead motherfucker.

No sooner than we stopped out the front of his run-down brick home, the door was opened and Maxwell ran out to meet us on his front lawn.

"I heard; I heard. It wasn't me. I had nothin' to do with your woman's death." He held his hands up and out in front of him, shaking them from side to side.

"Funny, Max, how in the fuck do you know what we were coming here for?" I asked.

"People talk, brother. I heard. She had a party and we fucked, but that was it. I left and she was fine."

Talon stepped forward. "This is not something we need to fuckin' talk about out in public. In the house, now," he ordered, and when that happened, people knew to follow.

Maxwell turned and led us up the concrete path to his house. Stoke, Pick and Killer stayed out front, while Blue, Talon and I entered. The stench of pot, mildew and pussy filled our noses.

"Damn, Maxwell, clean up the fuckin' place; it stinks in here," Blue said with his upper lip raised in a grimace.

Max laughed. "Yeah. Just been a busy time for me, brothers. Busy time. Got new whores I been testin' out; they're in some of the rooms. I'd be happy if you guys wanted to have a go at them."

I looked at *my* brothers, his no longer since he left the club, and saw they both held the look of disgust I knew I had.

Blue whispered something to Talon, who nodded in return, and then I watched Blue walk to the front door. In the next second, Pick was in the house and heading down the corridor to the left. He was paying the whores a visit with, no doubt, a little warning.

Talon walked over to the kitchen table, and in one sweep of his arms, everything on it fell to the floor in a loud clatter. He leaned his arse against it and said with a chin lift, "Max, come and have a seat. Griz has some questions, but I have something to say first." Talon waited until Maxwell was seated in the seat closest to him. He waited until Maxwell looked up at him, and then he took a breath, glared and said, "You no longer have the right to call us brothers. You left the club to deal with your whores and, I guess, run your fuckin' life down the shit hole, but that was your choice. So you live by it."

"All right, sure. Okay, bro—sir...um, Talon."

We all laughed at how pathetic he was.

Pick cleared his throat behind all of us. We turned, he gave a chin lift and then he left the house. It was the all-clear for us to do what we had to, meaning—the whores were too high to know what was going on.

I walked over to the table and stood just in front of Maxwell.

"Tell me, Max; why in the fuck would you have a party at my ex's *while* my daughter was in the same damned house?" I bellowed in his face.

"Look, man, I-I...shit! She...she needed some extra money. So, you know, I paid her for the night to fuck some customers, and then before we left...I had a go with her."

"*You pimped her out while my child was there?*" I roared. Someone grabbed me from behind, because they knew I was ready to jump this fucker and rip his worthless head off.

"Why'd she need money, Max? Griz was giving her

enough to help with the cost of their kid," Talon asked.

"Um, shit. Ah…your woman—"

"She ain't my woman, but she was still the fuckin' mother of my child, so talk, dickface," I growled. Blue let go of me and stepped back. He took out his phone, flipped it open and hit record. It was the same process we took every time we questioned anyone for anything.

"All right, okay. You see, she—ah, she got to like…a bit of crack."

I grabbed him by his dirty white tee and pulled him up so our faces were only inches apart and his feet dangled off the ground.

"You meanin' to tell me you sold crack to my ex?"

"Fuck no, man. I don't deal with that shit—I promise, but...my new partner does."

I threw him back into his chair and turned my back on him. "Tell me who."

"I can't, Griz. I can't; he'll kill me. He's one mean motherfucker."

Blue snorted. "And we won't kill you if you don't tell us?"

"Hell, please don't do this."

"Enough," Talon growled. "Max, they're selling crack in our territory. They will be dealt with, so just give us his name," Talon barked.

"Whatever you do, he'll want payback."

"We'll see," Blue said.

"Shit. All right, but it didn't come from me. Can you promise me that?"

"Sure, Max. Sure." Talon smirked.

Fuckin' dipshit. Did he not see Blue recording this?

"His name's Ryan Little, and he lives over in Delecombe."

"Thanks, mate. We'll figure out the rest." Talon stood tall and pulled his gun—with a silencer—from his back holster and pointed it at Maxwell's head.

Max raised his hands and cried, "Wait, wait! Please, please don't kill me. I told you who it was. I told you!"

Talon lowered his gun and sighed. "I guess that's true." He nodded to himself. In the next second, he fired his gun and hit Max in the left knee. As Maxwell screamed, Talon picked up a cloth from the floor and stuffed it into his mouth. "That's for lettin' this shit happen in the first place. No one brings crack into my territory. Pass the word on." He stood tall, turned and walked toward the front door, but I hadn't moved. "Griz, brother," Talon called. "Do what you want." He glanced over his shoulder and walked out of the house with Blue following.

In his haste to get away, Maxwell fell to the floor shaking and holding his knee, still moaning in pain from the gunshot wound. I raised my foot and planted it in the side of his head. He fell to his side, whimpering like some lost little kid.

"You really should have never crossed me and my family, even if she was my ex. But what broke the respect I still had for you, was the fact you were stupid enough to do shit around my child. That—I can never forgive."

It was my turn to remove my gun, which was also prepared with a silencer on the end, from my side holster. I aimed at Maxwell and fired a round into his other knee, and then another into his left arm. As I watched him roll around in pain, I smiled. At least the fucker, who played with not only the brotherhood, but my family, now knew not to.

I leaned over and hissed, "Keep the fuck outta trouble, Maxwell, or we will be back, and you know what will happen then. If I see your face again, there'll be a bullet between your eyes."

Before parting, I fired another shot into his stomach. Hopefully he'd die before his whores found him.

Deanna

After being at work for an hour, I was, for once, enjoying the silence. I loved working here. I loved the smell of the books and watching what people chose to read. But on some days, the silence did get to me...only not today.

In the last twenty-four hours, I'd had my fill of noise, tension and company—well, except maybe Grady and Swan's.

Oh, well, would you fuckin' look at that? I counted Swan in the mix of things.

Strange.

The library doors opened and a regular came in. I was sure she was here every day—at least, every day I worked she was. Someone always accompanied her in, holding her arm and then seating her at a table with some audiobooks to listen to. It had taken me my second day of seeing her a month ago to realise she was blind, and the person who helped her in here had to be her sister. They looked alike in many ways. Both were slim, tall and red-haired, only the blind one's hair was shorter, styled in a pixy cut, where her sister had long hair, which was usually plaited down her back.

The only thing that annoyed the hell outta me was the way the one who wasn't blind would speak to her sister. It was like she was the dirt under her fingernail she wanted to get rid of. It took all my strength to not say anything.

What also annoyed me was the fact it was obvious the bitch sister had advised the other on what to wear. Where the bitch looked immaculate—perfect hair, light green eyes, flawless make-up and designer clothes—the blind one always wore tracksuit pants, baggy tees or hooded jumpers. Her hair was always scruffy-looking, like she'd just gotten out of bed.

The bitch left with a glare, and like every day I saw it, I wanted to go over and find out what in the hell was going on, but I had enough of my own shit to deal with, rather than adding someone else's to the mix.

One day I would, or I'd never forgive myself.

It was after lunch, and I was working the floor, replacing the returned books to their shelves when the front automatic doors swished open, and in walked Julian. He always looked good; today he wore a red polo shirt with dark blue jeans and black leather boots. I watched him scan the front desk and then the floor. When he spotted me, a smile lit his face and he bounced on over.

"Hello, bitch-face," he said stopping in front of me.

I sent an eye roll his way and turned back to the shelf. "Afternoon, cum-sucker. What brings you here?"

He giggled, but then it abruptly stopped. I looked at him to see he was studying me.

Oh, crap, what's going to come out of his mouth now?

He gasped. "No way."

"What?"

"O-M-G, no way." He pulled his phone from his back pocket and dialled a number. "Hey, sugarplum, you know how I was going to the library to see how our Deanna was after last night and being blindsided by what she was going home to?" He waited for an answer. "Yes, well, I'm here and guess what I see...our woman's glowing like she got some nom-nom last night!" he squealed.

"Julian," I growled.

"I know," he screeched. "Hang on; I'll put you on

speaker." He clicked a button and held out his phone.

"Deanna Drake," Zara's excited voice called out. "Tell me now what went on last night, and tell me why you haven't called me already to tell me what happened last night. Hun, I should have been the first one to be told. Holy cow, babe! Finally—you and Griz! This is soooo awesome. Oh, wow. I can't believe this. I'm so excited for you. Was it good? Did he treat you right?"

"Up-the-duff, if you'd let her actually speak, you'll hear what she has to say," Julian said.

I sighed. "You losers will have to wait for the juicy details. I'm at work, and this is not the place to be talking about these things."

"Deannaaaa," Zara whined, but Julian pressed a button again and held it back up to his ear.

"Baby Maker, I see the seriousness in her eyes. She's not gonna budge. What? Oh, oh, good idea. Okay, I'll see you soon." He ended the call and turned to me. "She'll be here when you finish up; we're going for a coffee down the road. This is exciting; I can't wait to hear it all," he gushed, and then he turned, grabbed a book and walked over to the table where the blind woman sat.

I looked at the clock that sat above the attending desk and saw I had two hours left of work before the cheer crew wanted all the details. It wasn't that I didn't want to share, but I also didn't want to jinx what had happened with Grady. Maybe if I said it out loud it could change things. Though, I also knew they wouldn't give up without hearing everything.

Damn.

As soon as the clock hit four, Julian was up at the front desk smiling like he'd just given a head-job to his favourite actor. After clocking off, I walked around the desk and toward the front door.

"Zara said she would meet us at the coffee place. She just has to drop the monsters off with Mattie and Swan, and then she'll be here. Oh, and do you know that gorgeous woman I was sitting with is blind?"

"Yes."

"I think she was really scared to talk to me at first, but then—you know how everyone loves me—she ended up opening up and talking back."

"What's her deal?" I asked as we walked down the road.

"She has to come to the library every day while her sister works, because it isn't safe at home for her. I asked her what she meant by that, and she said her sister doesn't trust she's capable at home on her own. I called bullshit and told her that. Sure, she may be blind, but a lot of blind people live in their own houses and can easily take care of themselves."

Entering the coffee house, we found a seat to wait for Zara; although it wasn't hard, since the place was quiet with only a few business people scattered around.

"I've seen her sister, and she seems like a real bitch." Julian raised an eyebrow at me. "A bigger bitch than me, even. Always bossing her around, never smiles...I don't know; I wouldn't trust her sister. She needs to get out of that situation."

"That's what I said, but she won't. She said she has no money and her sister takes care of all that by working."

"Maybe we can see what we..." I trailed off as I spotted a person in the far corner. "How long has Billy been following us?"

Billy was the youngest member in the Hawks Motorcycle Club...or as Zara would call him, the cookie-lovin' biker.

"Oh, he was out the front when I arrived."

"Dammit, Grady's already got people following me and Jason isn't even out of jail yet."

"Who's Grady? O-M-G, that's Griz, isn't it? I never

knew his real name, but that is so hot for him. Why doesn't he go by that all the time?"

"Not sure," I said and sent a glare to Billy, who ignored it.

"Give the kid a break. He's only doing what he's been told."

"Exactly."

"Honey, don't be too hard on Grady. Isn't it obvious he just wants to keep you safe? I think it's sweet, actually."

"I guess," I grumbled. In retrospect, I knew I shouldn't be upset by it, but it had kinda put a downer on my good mood. *Grady had better make it up to me tonight.*

The front door opened, and Zara, in a long skirt and black tee walked—okay, waddled was more like it—in. She spotted us, clapped and ran-slash-swayed over. It was a funny sight to see.

"Hoo-wee, I can't wait. Spill! Spill now, woman."

"Can't I get a coffee first?" I smiled.

"Sure." Zara grinned, and then called over her shoulder, "Billy, can you get us two lattes and a hot chocolate, please?"

I rolled my eyes.

"Sure, Wildcat," Billy said with a deeper voice than I expected.

"Now you can talk."

"I don't want to go gettin' your hopes up or anything; this thing with Grady—"

"Oh, wow, you're on first name basis? It's serious!" Zara gushed, interrupting me.

Another eye roll from me. "But...you know things could change. I know I'm not the easiest person to get along with." Both of them snorted. "So it could all go to shit, and I worry if I act like a woman and rave about how last night was the best night in a long time for me...yeah, I just worry."

"Hun," Zara started and placed her hand over mine. "Live in the moment. We can both see the shine in your eyes—a shine that has been lost for a long time—coming back, and it only happened after what occurred with you and Griz last night."

"And if anyone can put up with Satan herself, it would be hot-man Griz," Julian added.

"He's right, Deanna. Griz has had his eye on you for-freakin' ever, and I don't know how, but he finally got over the age difference and took what he's wanted since you walked into his life."

"I think he held that pause button of his, because it also had a lot to do with his psycho ex. May she rest in peace,"

Julian said and crossed his chest in a silent prayer.

"But," Zara said, "he knows you are nothing like her. Nothing."

I looked over Zara's shoulder to Billy. He silently placed the drinks on the table. With a thank you from all of us, he gave a chin lift and left to go back to his seat across the room.

"Now, that's all sorted; spill the beans, woman." Julian grinned.

Lifting the warm cup to my lips, I took a sip to hide my smile. They were right; I had to live in the moment, and if Griz hadn't run already from the way I was, then I guess I was lucky and I'd run with what we had—whatever that was.

Placing the cup back down on the table, I cleared my throat. "Okay, last night I went to bed after finding out Grady had not only moved himself in, but Swan as well." I turned a glare on Zara. "And by the way, thanks for the heads up—*not.*"

"Oh, pfft. I think I know what the outcome was, so I'm glad I did it."

"Anyway, I went to bed in a state of shock as Grady was putting Swan down to sleep. I expected him to sleep with her in her room or the other spare one, and then my thoughts started running wild—"

"Like how such a hot piece of male was only metres away and you wanted to jump his bones? Well, one for certain." Julian cackled and then sobered. "Wait, should we be talking about this in front of..." He gestured with his head to Zara.

"What do you mean? Of course I can hear this," Zara snapped.

"Not you, the babies. Should we get some ear-muffs and place them on your belly to block all this out?"

Zara and I looked at each other and cracked up laughing.

"Whatever, mofos. Fine, corrupt the young; see if I care."

"I love that you do care, Julian, but I promise they won't remember anything being said here." Zara smiled warmly at him.

I took a breath and continued, "As I was saying, I was making myself horny, so I pulled out Vinny, but just when I was about to get into it, my door opened, and in walked Grady."

Zara covered her mouth, though I'd already seen the huge smile she was trying to hide behind her hand. While Julian gestured with his hands for me to keep going, his eyes shone with glee.

"I asked him why he was there and he said he was tired. I said there were other places to sleep, and he told me to be quiet, because he was exhausted. He got into bed and I thought *fuck it*, and continued on with what I was doing."

"Oh, no, you didn't." Julian laughed.

"Wow," Zara said, her eyes as big as saucers.

I grinned widely and said, "I did. He freaked, jumped out of bed and was over on the other side of the room in seconds."

They both laughed with me.

"Then what?" Zara asked, leaning forward as much as she could with her round belly.

"I kept going and asked him to join me. He said no, but I could tell he wanted to by the large tent he had going on in his boxers." I smiled at the thought. "After a while, he ended up shovin' his boxers down and said 'two can play at that game', *and then* he started to tug his chain."

"Holy crap, that is so hot," Julian moaned, and Zara nodded in agreement.

"In the end, he couldn't resist any longer and came over to give me the best head-job I've ever had. I swear, I would have seen angels singing above my head if my eyes were open."

"Yippee!" Zara clapped and wiggled in her seat.

"Aaaand?" Julian asked.

I giggled like an actual girly woman as I teased, "I wanted to finish him...but..."

"But what?" Julian screamed. Zara shushed him.

"He'd already finished. Apparently, just going down on me had him so worked up, he'd pounded his spunk onto my bed."

"Shit. Oh...damn. I need a fan or I need to come." Julian sighed and leaned back in his chair.

"That is soooo cool." Zara beamed, and I beamed right back at her.

It *was* totally cool, and I couldn't wait to do it again, even if he had teased me that morning and left me wanting him more than anything all day long. I mean, of course he would pay for it; he *had* to pay for it. I'd been so soaking wet all day, that I shoulda brought an extra pair of underwear.

Great, now it was even worse just thinkin' about what the night might entail.

Griz

My body hummed with anticipation; I needed to get home to my woman, take her in my arms and then plant my cock inside her.

Especially after the day I had. Going from Maxwell's house, Talon called reinforcements in after we found where Ryan Little lived, and travelled our way to his place in Delecombe. It was only seconds after we pulled up to his two-storey home when another ten brothers pulled their own Harleys up and surrounded the jackass's house.

The little, bald, fat prick was smug enough to let us in. He had about eight men who sat, stood or leaned around the living room as we talked about what we wanted. The choice we gave him was either he stopped dealing in our territory, or he'd end up a dead man. He laughed and said he'd consider it. Then the dick turned to me and informed me that since my woman was dead, the money she'd clocked up using *his* drugs now fell on me.

That was when all hell broke loose. The fight was bound to happen; it was just sooner than we thought. Talon stood by my side as I beat the shit outta Ryan and told him he'd never see his money. The other brothers each fought their own battle against Ryan's men.

Once things calmed down, we left the house with a promise it'd be worse if we found out he was still around and dealing.

We all went back to the compound to clean up and have a sit down. It was decided to keep a close eye on the fucker; we needed to know what his next move would be, if he was game enough to even make one. But I was sure he'd be shittin' himself right now and packing himself up to leave town. If he didn't, the fucker was just asking for a bullet.

After the meeting ended, I rode my Harley to Wildcat's place, where I'd left my vehicle and daughter that morning. Talon had ridden next to me, keen to get home to his wife and kids, but once we arrived, she was nowhere in sight. Instead, Mattie had the tribe of kids in the living room playing and watching TV. I could see Swan had taken a liking to Maya, as they were playing with some weird looking dolls.

"Where is she?" Talon asked Mattie.

"Zara and Julian are with Deanna having a pow-wow."

Talon laughed. "Shit, brother, you're fucked," he said to me.

I rolled my eyes and shrugged. I didn't care what Deanna told the other two, as long as she was happy when I saw her next.

The front door swung open, and Zara stood there with a frown upon her face. My heart picked up, and worry took over my body.

I took a step toward her and barked, "What's wrong?"

She looked at me quickly, and then back at Talon. "Did I just hear you swear in front of the kids?" she scolded.

Worry slipped from my body and I chuckled.

Fuck. I had been so wound up, my chest hurt. I rubbed at it.

"Dad's gonna get it," Cody chimed in behind us from the couch.

"Shut it, Cody," Talon said.

"Talon Marcus, don't you tell Cody to shut it; tell me instead—did you just swear in front of the kids?"

He rolled his eyes and sighed, looking like he was praying for patience. "Kitten," he growled with a tone of warning.

"Don't *Kitten* me, and don't do it again, Talon, or you will get a tongue lashing in front of the kids, *again*." She moved forward and Julian stepped in behind her; he closed the door and turned, and then looked at me blushing.

What. The. Fuck?

"It won't be me gettin' the tongue lashing tonight," Talon said with a lift of his eyebrow.

"Jesus, Dad! I'm here, ya know, and I know what you mean. Gross!"

Talon hit Cody in the back of the head and stalked to Zara. He pulled her into his arms, whispered something in her ear and she melted into him.

"Just don't swear again," she said. "Also, you can't talk like that in front of them." She bit her bottom lip worriedly.

"How can I help it when my woman is so fu—freakin' hot?"

"Don't think you can charm your way out of this." She turned in his arms and her eyes fell on Cody. "Cody Marcus."

"Uh-oh," Cody uttered.

"If I hear you use that J-word once again, I will wash

your mouth out with soap. You hear me, boy?"

"You sound like Grandma when you say that."

Shit.

Zara hated being referenced with her mum. Though she loved her mother, even Zara thought she was bat-shit crazy at times.

Zara gasped. "Cody Anthony Marcus! You take that back."

"Now *you're* gonna get it," Talon sang, and then laughed when Zara elbowed him in the stomach.

Cody stood up with wide eyes. Damn, he was a tall kid for a thirteen-year-old. "Sorry! I didn't mean it. Sorry, Mum."

Zara's hand went to her mouth, her eyes welled with tears and she sobbed.

Hell, that kid knew how to work it. It was the first time he'd called her mum, and he'd just saved his arse from gettin' into deeper shit by doing it. I was sure Zara knew it, and I could see Talon knew it from the proud smile on his face, but both of 'em didn't care at all.

Mattie and Julian had somehow disappeared and I didn't even want to think about what they were doing. It was my turn to head out as well to let Talon and his family have this moment, while I went home to my woman and had my own moment.

I picked up Swan from the floor, kissed a usually-loud Maya on the forehead as she silently watched her new brother and parents with warm eyes, and then walked to the door.

"I'm out," I said to the room.

They all turned to me; I thought I'd escape without an incident, but Zara ran over to me, pulled me and Swan into her arms and cried, "Oh, Griz, thank you, thank you for bringing my best friend back to me." Shit, with the amount of tears leaking outta her, my shoulder was getting wet.

"Uh, sure." I looked over her head to Talon. He shrugged and said, "Pregnancy makes her crazy."

Zara spun around. "Oh, shush it." She looked over at Cody and must have remembered what he'd just said before I'd announced I was leaving. She sniffled and ran over to the poor kid, bringing him in close and hugging the shit outta him.

"Dad," Cody whined, though anyone could tell he was happy.

"Good luck with that," I said with a chuckle, not only to Cody, but to Talon as well, and then left.

I lifted Swan into my car and onto her seat, and after strapping her in, I smiled down at her. "Did you have a good day, baby?"

She looked up at me and smiled. I could see her brain tickin' something over in her mind and then in the next second, she blew me away. "H-home."

"Yes, sweetheart, we're going home to Deanna." I kissed her head, closed the door and took a breath to get myself under control. I needed to get home to my woman.

Deanna

I noticed the house was dark and quiet when I pulled into the drive. I'd thought Grady would've been back by now, especially when he had Swan to think of. Then I wondered if they'd eaten...and if I should make something for dinner.

Well, have a fuckin' look at me. I'm all Betty homemaker, thinkin' of the family. I chuckled to myself.

I was just about to put the key in the lock when Billy called out from behind me, telling me to wait. I bit my tongue so I wouldn't argue. Yes, it had hurt me to do so, but I didn't want him to get chewed out by Grady.

So instead of me entering the house first, Billy made his way in and told me to wait outside. Five minutes later, he came back out and told me it was all clear.

With an eye roll, I said, "Thanks. Um...do you want to come in?"

His eyes widened. "Ah, no thanks. Griz would kick my arse if I did." That didn't explain why he looked so shocked when I had asked him.

Shrugging, I replied, "Okay." I then turned and shut the door behind me.

After changing into jeans and a plain red tee, I went downstairs and looked through the cupboards and fridge for something to eat...for everyone.

It didn't take long to see I had to do a shopping trip for groceries the next day, but I was lucky enough to find all the ingredients for chow-mein.

The pot was boiling by the time I heard the front door unlock and two steady, heavy booted feet made their way into the kitchen. I looked behind me and my heart sped up at the sight of Grady holding Swan in his arms, both of them smiling at me.

"Hey." I grinned.

"How you doing, darlin'?"

Damn, that sounded nice. A thrill was sent straight to my core. "Good." I nodded. "Dinner is nearly ready." I looked at the clock above the fridge; it was just about six-thirty. "You guys must be hungry, eh?"

Grady sat Swan in her seat that was attached to a kitchen chair at the table. He rounded the counter and pulled me into his arms.

"Dinner would be great. Next time, I'll be home earlier so Swan's not eating so late. Yeah?"

Home.

Fuck. He'd said home.

I thumped my forehead against his chest so he wouldn't see what that one word had done to me. I hated anyone seeing I was becoming mushy, but I was.

Fuck it, I *really* was. Stupid cocksucking emotions.

"Dee?"

"Home early would be great," I muttered into his chest.

He gave me a squeeze and pushed me back, his eyes searching mine and his grin widening. "Good, now kiss me."

"Grady," I hissed and looked at Swan, who was watching us with her adorable, little head tilted to the side.

"She won't care, but I will if I don't have your mouth on mine in a second."

After a sigh, I was ready to argue the point, until his lips met mine in a demanding kiss. Forgetting everything, I wrapped my arms around his neck and pulled him close.

"H-home," I heard a soft whisper say.

I moved back a step and gazed at Swan in wonder. Had she really just said that?

Grady moved in behind me, wrapping his arms around my waist, and his chin rested on my shoulder as he whispered, "She shocked the shit outta me when we were leaving Wildcat's place and she said the same thing. She likes it here, darlin'."

I nodded, fighting my damn emotions once again. "W-well." I cleared my throat. "I had better get dinner finished. Why...um, why don't you get Swan ready for bed, and by then everything will be done?"

He must have known I needed the distraction from the situation at hand, because he moved from me with a pat on the arse and a look that read there was more of that to come later, as he went to Swan and took her to get changed.

I was in seriously deep shit.

Having people at the table in my own house for dinner was...overwhelming. Fuckin' tears, sobbing and screaming all wanted to leak from my body. Since I'd lost the Drakes, I'd never *felt* so much in one night, and never felt a connection to a family. Watching Grady and Swan together warmed me in so many ways.

I knew then I was one lucky bitch.

Sure, Zara had welcomed me into her family—her whole tribe had, and I was more than grateful for it—but even that was different to what was in front of me now.

Only, there was no way in hell I was turning into some *Meet the Cleavers* family.

"Dee?" Grady's voice grumbled beside me.

"Huh?"

"I'm gonna get Swan into bed and read to her for a few. Why don't you get ready for bed too?"

My body tingled with anticipation. From the heat and wetness I felt from my hoo-ha, I was more than ready for bed.

With a small nod and a bite on my bottom lip, I watched Grady's eyes darken. He stood, got Swan from her chair and placed her on her feet. She padded her small feet around the table to me, and before I knew what she was going to do, she wrapped her arms around my waist and hugged me tightly.

My heart shattered, only to be put back together wholly with a new, sweeter beat to it made by a certain little girl.

This time, there was no stopping the tears that pooled in my eyes. I bit my lip tighter and looked up at Griz; he was watching the whole thing with warm eyes and a beautiful smile brightening his face.

My hand on its own accord reached up to run down the back of her head. With that, she pulled away and started into the living room. I knew Griz was waiting for my eyes to reach his, but I couldn't give them. "There's only so much emotional crap this woman can take for the night. You'd better work it outta my body later."

A manly chuckle filled the room. "I'd be glad too."

Fuck. I looked up at him and asked, "I said that out loud?"

"Sure did."

"Great, now I'm turning into Zee."

With another laugh, he left the room to go see to his daughter.

Two hours later, I had cleaned the kitchen, filled the dishwasher, took a shower, got into my boy shorts and a cami and then changed the bed sheets.

Turning around from the bed, I was about to head back downstairs to grab a drink, but found Griz leaning against the doorframe.

"How's Swan?" I asked.

"Asleep. We played for a bit, I read her some books and she went out like a light."

"Good." I nodded. "That's good. She looked tired."

He stood straight and took a step forward. "I've decided we're all going out tomorrow." Another step forward, but the fiery look in his eyes had me backing up a step.

"Um, where?"

"Wildlife Park. Always wanted to take Swan there, have never gotten around to it. Now I will." Another step forward and he slipped his tee over his head.

I bit my lip to stop myself from groaning as I eye-raped his beautiful, muscular, tattooed chest.

I licked my lips and he watched my tongue. "Well, I'm sure Swan will enjoy that."

Another step and he was in front of me. "You're coming," he quirked an eyebrow and added, "in more ways than one, but tomorrow you are coming with us."

"But—"

"No buts, woman."

"Whatever." Now was not the time to argue; I needed, and so very fuckin' much wanted, his body to fill me *in more ways than one*. "Enough talk, let's fuck." I grinned up at him. His eyes were hooded and he sighed.

"No, darlin'. The way I'll make you feel, the way my body will possess yours, it's more than just fuckin'."

Holy hell.

"Okay, stud. Prove it."

He grinned wickedly at me. "Gladly."

Griz

I clenched my fists at my side once again. No matter how much my dick wanted inside her, I wouldn't allow it. I meant every word I'd just said. I wanted her to be fully aware of who she was about to have in her body, mind and soul.

"Take your clothes off. Now," I growled.

Her eyes widened. I was waiting for her to argue back, to tell me to get fucked, because I knew she hated being told what to do. Though, I also knew I was possibly the only one who could get away with it.

She removed her girly top and shorts quickly and quietly.

Yes, I was in there. She may not totally know it yet, but I was embedded deep in there.

Hiding my grin, I told her, "Get on the bed on all fours and face me."

"You're fuckin' lucky I'm in a good mood, Grady."

Hell. I loved it when she said my name. "I know," I admitted.

She climbed on top of the bed and turned so she was on her hands and knees facing me.

I took a step back, flipped the button on my jeans and then slowly slid down the zipper. She watched every move I made with an eager look upon her face. My jeans dropped to the floor with my boxers, and I kicked them off and stood before her.

My hand wound around my cock and started to stroke it. "I saw last night that you liked how I handle my dick. Am I right?"

"Grady," she groaned on an exhale.

I had been right, so I kept tuggin' myself, just out of reach in front of her. The sneaky woman ran her hands over her beautiful boobs, down her stomach to her pussy, which I knew would be wet for me.

"You keep touchin' your sweet spot, you won't get my cock."

She glared, but then pulled her hand away and rested it back down on the bed. "You had better give it to me *now* then, or I'll finish all this on my own."

I smirked. "Bullshit. Tell me you want my cock in your mouth."

"Grady," she said with a warning tone.

"Tell me," I growled.

She licked her lips. We both knew she wanted this, and if she didn't hurry the fuck up, I'd blow yet-a-fuckin'-gain too early from just thinking about how wet her pussy was.

"Babe, I want to suck, lick and devour your cock inside my mouth right now."

"Christ," I bit out and moved forward. With my hand in her hair, I slowly slid my rock-hard erection into her sweet mouth and groaned. "Shit that feels good." Pulling back out, I pushed in again quickly. She moaned, and the hum of it sent a pulse through my dick.

With a tighter grip on her hair, I pumped my cock into her mouth over and over again.

Hell. I had to stop, or I was gonna come.

Loosening my grip on her hair, I ordered, "Move." She did by sitting back on her knees. I got on the bed and laid flat. "I want you to fuck my face, darlin'."

Her breathing picked up and I knew she liked the

thought of that. She climbed over to me and positioned her snatch above my face, her knees on each side of my head. I grabbed her thighs and lowered her delicious-tasting pussy to my mouth. It didn't take her long to take control. She moved her hot body over my mouth, running her pussy back and forth over my tongue.

"Jesus, Grady, Jesus," she moaned. "Fuck, babe. I'm gonna come."

I pushed her up and barked, "No. Not fuckin' yet. Not until my cock is inside of you."

"Yes," she hissed and moved off my face to lay her head on her pillow.

"Wrong again, darlin'. Get up on all fours."

She smirked, but did as I asked...or I should say *told*. She flipped over and got up on her hands and knees once again. I crept up behind her, so fuckin' eager to have my cock deep within her tight core.

"Shit, tell me you're protected."

She nodded.

"I need to hear it, darlin'."

"I'm on the pill and clean. I've been tested, recently," she said over her shoulder, her lust-filled eyes upon mine.

"Thank fuck. So am I."

She laughed. "What, you're on the pill too?"

Little minx. I slapped her arse and she moaned loudly. "You know what I mean," I growled. "I'm clean." And with that, I forced my cock balls-deep straight into her, knowing her pussy would be wet and ready enough for me to take, and it was. Both of us hissed and groaned.

"Hell. I knew you'd feel good, but this is way fuckin' better than I fantasised." I pulled out and pushed back in over and over again.

"Damn, Grady. Christ, you feel so good in there. You belong inside me."

Shit.

"And don't ever forget it," I said through clenched teeth. I was close; there was no way I could hold off for much longer. The way her tight walls milked my cock—it was fuckin' bliss.

I reached over her, grabbed her shoulders and pulled her up so her back was to my chest, all while still pumping into her twat. As I held onto her with one arm across her chest, I reached with the other and found her clit with my fingers. She whimpered and put her arms above her head, reaching to the back of my neck to hold on.

"Fuck, darlin'. Tell me you're close." The more I played with her button, the wetter she became; I was sliding in and out of silk.

"I-I'm really close. Oh, God. Grady."

I picked up speed and pounded harder into her. On a scream, she came undone and cried out my name. Two hard thrusts later, I came right along with her as her walls still clenched around my cock.

Deanna

What the fuck?

Griz woke me up the next morning, ordering me to get me sweet arse outta bed so we could get to the Wildlife Park. My body was so relaxed I didn't even bite his head off, and I was excited to go somewhere with both of them. I had such great sleep I hadn't even heard Swan wake at—what Grady told me—seven that morning.

By 10am, everything had gone to shit...literary.

Grady had paid for us at the door. We got bags of food to feed the animals given to us as we walked in through a little gift shop, and now I gaped up at Grady, who was pushing Swan in her stroller. It was a damn hot sight—a biker man with tats, wearing a short-sleeved black tee, his club vest over it and tight-ass black jeans. I was ready to lie on the ground, spread my legs and beg to have his cock in me once again.

Damn, I had totally missed the point and gone Grady-crazy instead. But that could be understood, I was sure.

Back to how everything went to shit...it was when we walked outta the gift shop and entered the Wildlife Park, where kangaroos and God-knows-what-else ran wild. There was shit—their *shit*—everywhere.

Now, I was no prim-proper lady, but *there was shit!* *SHIT*, people—everywhere. I was scared.

"Suck it up, princess. It ain't that bad." Grady chuckled at my shocked, scared face.

"Grady, babe, I don't know where to step. Stuff it; you'll have to carry me. No, I've got it—I'll get in the stroller with Swan; she can sit on my knees."

That was when Grady burst out with a deep, manly laugh, which turned me the fuck on. How could a guy's laugh turn me on when I was surrounded by shit?

All right, okay, I may have over-exaggerated. There was shit everywhere, but once I saw how excited Swan was, I calmed my own freak-out down and watched as Grady let her out of the pram and walked with her over to the nearest kangaroo. He crouched down with Swan between his legs, and then proceeded to open the bag and show her how to place her hand out flat to feed the roo who had come right up to them.

The sight before me was amazing, and I wouldn't have changed it for anything else in the entire world.

"Dee," Grady called, "get over here."

I tentatively strolled over, worried I'd scare the roo away, but it took no notice of me. Grady grabbed my hand and pulled me gently down to crouch beside him. I looked down at Swan, and her smile of pure joy made my heart cry. She was beautiful.

Grady turned his head toward me and grinned. I knew my own smile matched his. It was fuckin' wonderful. He leaned over and placed his lips upon mine for a quick kiss.

Besides the crap everywhere, it had been the best day I'd had in such a long time. We saw crocodiles, emus, turtles and so much more. There were also koalas; one I actually held—after Grady pestered me to—for a photo.

We ate lunch at the cafe there, and then after that, we entered the snake enclosure—which freaked me the hell out, all while Grady and Swan got close, pointed, smiled, laughed and learned about the ugly-looking fuckers.

By the time we made it home in the late afternoon, I was sure not only Swan, but Grady, was just as tired as I was from walking around the thirty-seven some-odd acres of the wildlife park.

After I threw the shitty shoes out the back, I went to get changed before starting something for dinner. I was in my walk-in closet when Grady found me standing in my underwear, searching through my clothes for something comfortable to put on.

"How's Swan?" I asked. "I'm just gonna get changed and get some dinner on for us. I'm sure she'd need an early night after the amount of walking she's done today." I was bent over, going through my bottom drawers when I felt heat at my back. I turned my head to the side to see Grady's hungry eyes roaming my body. From the bulge in his jeans, I knew he liked what he saw.

In the next second, a gasp was pulled from my mouth as Grady's hand slid straight into my panties and into me.

"Fuck, darlin', how are you already wet?" he growled.

"Because I've been around you all day," I answered truthfully. I went to stand, but his other hand went to my shoulder to hold me down.

"Stay," he ordered.

Damn, his voice sent me wild. As his fingers slid in and out of me, he used his other hand to slowly pull my panties all the way down, and then before I could protest, he slapped my arse hard, ripping a moan from my throat. He

then kissed where he had slapped; he was driving me
insane and he knew it.

"W-where's Swan?"

"Downstairs, watchin' some girly cartoon show. So we
have to be quick." He turned, never removing or stopping
his fingers from fucking me senseless, switched on the light
and closed the door.

"Damn, you're beautiful," he said as he pulled his
fingers outta me, and they went straight into his mouth.
Groaning and growling while he sucked my juices off his
fingers, he used his other hand to undo his jeans and free
his cock.

He stepped up behind me and slapped my arse again
with both hands on both checks, causing another moan
from my lips to erupt. As he rubbed his palm over the sting,
he rubbed his cock through my wetness.

"Fuck, darlin', I can't wait any longer."

A whimper escaped me. I needed his dick inside of me
now, too.

He must have known this, because one hand
disappeared from my hip as he grabbed his dick and lined it
up with my centre. A scream tore outta me as he plunged
his thick rod balls-deep inside of me.

"Fuck, shh, princess. Shh."

"Grady, Jesus. God. That felt so good."

"Hell. Hold on to your ankles, darlin'. I won't let you fall, okay? But I gotta fuck you hard. So fuckin' hard. You trust me, right?"

Was he crazy? Of course I trusted him.

"Yes. Shit, yes."

"Thank Christ," he hissed. He pulled out of me and thrust back in hard and fast, but he didn't stop—he never stopped. He held onto my hips tightly as he entered me—in and out, over and over, again and again.

"God. Oh, fuck, Grady. Keep going. Don't stop."

His breath escalated, and I knew it wouldn't be long before he filled me with his seed. But that was okay, because the all-too-familiar tingle started in the base of my belly, going lower and lower until...

"Oh, oh. Hell. Yes. Yes, Grady."

"Damn. Fuck. Your sweet pussy is milking me, baby. Ah, fuuuck," he growled as he slammed into me one last time, filling me with his hot come.

With him still inside of me, he reached over and pulled my exhausted body up, so my back was to his chest. "That was fuckin' perfect. Tonight, we go slower. I can't wait to eat you out, darlin'. Do not shower before it; I wanna taste us inside you."

Holy hot, shit and damn—that was the fuckin' hottest thing anyone had ever said to me.

Griz

One week later

Sunday morning, I heard Swan making noises from down the hall. I turned my head to look at the clock on the bedside table. It was only six. Too fuckin' early, but I knew once she was fully awake, there was no stopping her. I looked down at Dee, who was curled up around my body. Her head was resting on my chest, an arm slung over my stomach and her legs were tangled around one of mine. I would've loved to wake her by fuckin' her hard and fast before Swan started crying, but there wouldn't have been time. Instead, I untangled myself; she sighed and shifted to roll on her other side.

She is so goddamn beautiful.

How in the fuck did I get so lucky?

And why in the hell did I spend so much time running from this, rather than takin' that leap and jumpin' straight into it with her?

Though, now that I thought about it, if we had fucked when I wanted—when she wanted—it wouldn't have worked out like it had. We were too fucked up back then. At least, I knew I was. I still had Kathy to deal with; there was no time for pussy besides one-night stands. I guessed that was also another reason I held off. I didn't want Deanna to be just a random one-night pussy. Maybe I knew she'd be more.

Fuckin' glad I waited. Even if it near killed me the time we went head-to-head in Wildcat's kitchen, when I'd ordered her to stay in my room at the compound.

A smile formed on my lips just thinkin' of it. She'd told me, 'You'll be tugging your chain every time you think of my arse.' And damn it if she wasn't right. I couldn't count the times I'd jacked off thinking of her—her mouth, her body, her attitude.

Ever since the time I was walkin' away and she'd called

me handsome.

I thought she was just teasing. Why in the hell would a young, hot bird like Deanna find me—an old, cranky guy— attractive. But the looks she'd given me and the small smiles told me that she was not shittin' me.

She did, in fact, want me, which shocked the shit outta me.

And now, here I was in a bloody relationship with her, and I couldn't be more fuckin' happy.

I moved my naked self from standing next to the bed, watchin' my woman like some trained puppy, to throwing on a tee and some cut-off track pants. After pissing and washin' my hands and face, I made my way down the hall to Swan's room.

When I opened the door, my eyes went straight to her crib. She was already standing up and smiling with a soft fabric doll in her hand.

"Mornin', sweetheart. You ready for some breakfast?"

She jumped up and down with her arms in the air, ready and waiting for me to grab her. I did, and in one swoop, I had my baby girl in my arms and we made our way downstairs. Once in the kitchen, I sat Swan on the bench next to me as I made her some porridge. It was her favourite—I would swear most kids thought it was gross;

my girl couldn't get enough of it. Fuck, I even hated the taste of it—reminded me of paste.

I grabbed the milk out of the fridge and noticed we needed some more. A grin came over me, caused by the thought of Deanna, Swan and myself walking through a supermarket together as a family. That was something we had to do today.

After I'd finished getting Swan's breakfast and tested that it wasn't too hot for her, I sat the bowl with a spoon in front of her and kissed her on the forehead. She smiled up at me. I could honestly say these past few days were the happiest I'd ever seen my daughter. Even with Kathy, it'd been like she was too scared to do anything, never feeling secure enough to open up and be what I thought normal kids were like. Here though, she was more out there, full of smiles, touches and happiness. I reckoned it had a lot to do with the atmosphere, because Deanna was so…bright—not that I'd ever say that to her face—though it wasn't just that. She'd welcomed us into her house—after we forced our way in, of course—and now if felt like this was our home.

Thinking of Deanna, I got the coffee pot ready, because I knew how much of a bitch my princess could be if she didn't have coffee as soon as her feet hit the kitchen. Thank fuck we weren't outta that, but we'd still have to stock up.

"Dadda," Swan called. I turned from staring out the kitchen window to see that Swan had finished her meal and was waiting for me to get her out of her chair.

"You had enough, baby girl?" When she nodded, I shoved the bowl away, pulled her chair back and lifted her into my arms. "We'd better get you dressed," I said with a kiss on her cheek.

As we were walking out of the kitchen, through the living area and to the hall that lead to the stairs, there was a knock on the front door.

I turned back and called, "Who is it?" but it probably came out more like an annoyed snap.

"The man of your dreams."

Fuck. Julian was here; it was too early for this shit. I liked the guy, but…yeah…he could be a bit much. I mean, there was no way in hell I'd ever say anything. The women loved him, and we'd—meaning me and Talon—get the shit kicked outta us if we ever tried to change him in any way. It wasn't that we were worried they'd literally kick the shit out of us…it was more that we were concerned they'd cut us off from their pussies. That could never fuckin' happen.

"Hello, sweetmeat!" he called through the door. I hurried to open it in case the neighbours thought I was havin' it off with him. Very fuckin' unlikely though—they knew I was here for my woman…but still.

Flicking the lock and opening the door, I was greeted by a grinning Julian and a quiet Mattie.

"Yo," I said.

"Oooooh, look at you, beautiful." My eyes went to Julian as he squealed this, just to make sure he was talking to my daughter and not me. Thank Christ, his excited face was directed at Swan. He clapped his hands out to her, and she was more than willing to be taken by him.

What was it with women and kids? They fuckin' adored this guy.

He pushed his way in, and I had to back up or he would've rubbed himself against me. Mattie followed behind him and gave me an apologetic gaze, but anyone could see he also adored the guy—in more ways than one.

Something I would not even think about.

"Sorry to come by so early; is Deanna still in bed?" Mattie asked.

"Not anymore, with all the bloody noise." She walked out of the hall and into the living room in hot fuckin' short-shorts and a light blue tee. My dick strained to get to her.

"Oops. Sorry, blossom. I didn't know you were in the room," she said as she walked up to Swan in Julian's arms and gave her a sweet peck on the cheek. Swan beamed up at her.

"Princess," I growled. I wanted—no, *needed*—her mouth on me as soon as my eyes caught sight of her each morning.

With an eye roll, she walked over to me. I wrapped her up in my arms and kissed the fuck outta her. She was finally getting used to doin' it in front of an audience.

She turned in my arms with a slight blush on her cheeks and met the guys' gazes.

"You do know that we're gay, right? So you don't need to mark your territory in front of us," Julian teased.

Deanna laughed. "He isn't doing it for you; it's what he wants, and if he doesn't get a kiss every morning, he gets cranky."

Mattie chuckled, and Julian smiled and said, "That is so awesome."

"What are you guys doin' here?" I left out *so fuckin' early.*

"We wanted to take Swan to see Zara and the kids. Is that okay?" Mattie asked.

Deanna looked up at me and raised her eyebrow. I shrugged. "If it's okay with Swan," I told the men.

"Do you wanna go, sweetheart?" Deanna asked her. Swan nodded. "Then you can go. Do you have a seat in the car for her? If not, you can borrow ours. She can't go in a car without a seat; it's unsafe…what?" she snapped at the end, after she noticed all of us smiling widely at her.

"Just happy to see you caring for Swan," I said and then looked at Mattie, "And you can take my car." I looked back down to Deanna, "We're taking yours to the supermarket; we need shit for the house."

"Oh, okay," she mumbled.

"Great!" Julian grinned. "Let's go get this monster organized for a day with her uncles, and then we'll get out of your hair. I'm sure you'll like that." He chuckled when Deanna gave him the finger after Swan turned her head away.

"I'll help," she said and followed Julian to the hall door, no doubt heading up to Swan's bedroom to get her dressed.

While they did that, Mattie and I went into the kitchen to shoot the shit about random stuff. Now *he* was more than normal, and very easy to get along with. Look, I didn't give a fuck if a person was gay or anything, but sometimes Julian just shoved the fact in your face and flirted shamelessly; Mattie didn't. He was quiet, and just sat back and watched what was goin' on around him. I supposed Julian was damned lively enough for the both of them.

"Mattie," Julian called from the front. I walked with him out into the living room to see Swan was now freshly dressed and lookin' happy. I walked over, gave her a kiss on the cheek and said, "Be a good girl."

"Oh, I will, but only if you kiss me." Julian smiled. *Jesus.*

"Never gonna happen, and you know if my daughter is harmed in any way in your care, I'll come for blood."

"Grady, stop it. She'll be fine; won't you, sweet girl?" Dee cooed and gave her a kiss on the cheek of her own. Swan nodded, waved and left along with a final farewell from both Mattie and Julian.

"You know, the more you cringe and react, he'll keep being over the top," Deanna explained as we watched them place Swan in my car.

"I highly doubt that. No one could knock that shit outta him; it's just who he is."

She laughed. "Yeah, that's true. Now, are we going back to bed to fuck?" She turned in my arms and raised her chin to look up at me with hooded eyes.

My hands went to her arse and I gave it a pinch. She hit me in the ribs. "I'd love to be buried inside of you right now, but we gotta go do some shopping. After we get home though, there will be nothing to stop me from having my cock in you."

She rolled her eyes. "You say such sweet things."

I chuckled. "And you love it." Her eyes turned serious as soon as 'love' left my lips. I wanted more than anything to tell her I loved her with everything I had, but we just weren't ready yet.

She closed her eyes, smiled, and then whispered, "Maybe." With that, she moved from my arms and stalked into the kitchen, her hips swaying in a way that had my cock hardening once again.

We weren't ready yet, but it was coming soon. Very fuckin' soon.

Deanna

I could not believe I was in a supermarket, with my man, shopping like some average Joe. It shocked the shit out of me that he wanted to go food shopping with me in the first place. Though, I knew as soon as I saw him walkin' down the aisles pushing a trolley, the sight would make me wet and I'd want to jump his bones. And it did. My hard, grey-eyed man with salt-and-pepper hair, tattooed arms, wearing biker boots, jeans and a black tee looked more than fuckin' hot in a supermarket pushing a trolley and collecting food to feed his family.

I went up behind him while he studied a package of pasta, wrapped my arms around his waist and stood on my tippy-toes to whisper in his ear, "I am so wet and ready for you; it's ridiculous."

A soft growl erupted from his chest. "Do not fuck with me right now or I'll take you on the floor right here and right now. I don't give a fuck who watches." His lips crashed down onto mine. I hated public displays of affection, but when it came to Grady, I didn't give a fuck.

"Deanna?" I heard over my shoulder. I was pissed someone had interrupted our make-out session, but when I turned around my stomach dropped, and I knew some shit was about to go down. There stood one of my exes, Nate Derick. He and I went out for six months just before Zara and her stuff went down. I broke it off with him because he wanted to get serious and I didn't. There was also the fact he wasn't that great in bed, but I wasn't a big enough bitch to say anything. He still looked good with his sandy-coloured hair, dark blue eyes, and his tall, slim body. He wore black trousers and a white shirt, dressed to impress like usual, and I supposed he had to for his job as the owner of a car dealership.

"Nate, um…hi," I said.

"It's great to see you, Deanna. I've been thinking about you heaps." *Oh, shit.* I felt Grady tense behind me. "Who's this? Your dad?" *Oh, fuck.* "Hi, I'm Nate, Deanna's ex…for now." He grinned and then held out his hand to Grady, who stood as still as a statue behind me.

"Are you fuckin' shittin' me?" Grady growled low and deep.

Nate straightened, put his hand down at his side—*thank God or he would have lost it*—and with a puzzled look, he asked, "About what?"

Instead of answering, Grady glanced down at me and asked, "Is this dickhead for real?"

I licked my lips.

"Excuse me, but what is your problem?" Nate snapped.

Holy crap.

Grady took a step forward, bringing me with him because I stood in front of him. "My problem, assface, is that you have the balls to ask if I'm her daddy when I was not even a second ago sucking her face and she was enjoying every minute of it. Now, did that look to you like I'm her fuckin' father?"

"Well, I just presumed you could have been an affectionate family, because it didn't make sense to me that Deanna would be interested in someone so old, when she could have someone like me."

Jesus Christ. Blood was about to be spilt.

Grady's eyes widened, turned to me and he barked, "And you let this fuckhead inside of you?" He seemed sick by the idea.

"Do *not* look at me like that, Grady Daniels. God knows where your cock has been, so don't fuckin' start judging me," I snapped with my hands on my hips, glaring up at him. How dare he?

"Deanna, I'm sure you can do better than this; this guy isn't worth it," Nate said from behind me. I felt him take a step closer and place a hand on my arm. "I'll get you out of here, if you like."

I closed my eyes as soon as a vicious hiss started coming from the direction of my furious biker boyfriend. "You take your goddamn hand off my woman or I will kill you."

"Who in the hell do you think you are?" Nate spat.

"You'll soon fuckin' find out *if* you do not remove your hand."

I'd had enough. We were starting to attract attention— okay, I was being naïve; we attracted attention as soon as Grady bellowed out that first time.

I shrugged out of Nate's hold, turned and leaned my back against Grady. Even if he had pissed me right the fuck off, there was no way I was letting some guy from my past look down on him or speak to him like shit, because Grady was my future.

"Nate, you need to get lost. You knew Grady wasn't my father, but you had to come over and act all tough and big to see if you could win me over. What you don't know is that Grady may be an arse and piss me the hell off, but I care for him. He is more of a man than you could ever be." He went to argue, but seriously, enough was enough. I held up my hand in front of me. "Don't. I really don't want to hear anything else from you. You need to leave."

He glared. "Deanna, you don't know what you're talking about. You'll regret going with him and not walking out with me. One day you'll come crawling back, and I don't know if I'll want you then."

This guy was deluded. I hadn't seen him in for-fucking-ever, and now he wants to cause this shit? What in the hell had come over him? I knew he never liked to lose, but this was plain stupid.

I sighed and decided to play dirty to get this jerk away from me. "Nate, I never did introduce you to my man…who gives me orgasm after orgasm. Nate, meet Griz, the Vice President of the Hawks Motorcycle Club."

His eyes widened, his face visibly paling in front of us. I heard Grady chuckle behind me. Nate took a step back, and then another.

"I-I…"

"Yeah, fuck off, dickhead, and if you ever sniff around my woman again, you'll pay the price," Griz growled, not caring if anyone around us heard him.

Nate spun around and stalked off. I was surprised I didn't see a wet patch on his pants; I was sure he'd shit himself.

Grady pulled my back closer to his front with an arm around my waist, and with his head on my shoulder, he uttered, "Bloody idiot."

I stepped away, turned around and glared. "Grab what we need for now. I want to leave."

He looked shocked by my hard tone. "Princess?"

"I do not want to have this conversation at the fuckin' supermarket in front of everyone. I want to go home."

"Fine."

I knew by his sharp tone that he thought he'd done nothing wrong, but he had; I was pissed enough to know he had. Sure, Nate was a dick, but I didn't need it thrown in my face that he had been inside of me in front of not only Nate, but other people as well. We both had people in our past I was sure we regretted, but the way Grady said it was as though I was scum. He was disgusted by it, and that fuckin' hurt.

So as soon as we got home, after a silent ride in the car

the whole way, I let him have it, and his reply was, "I didn't like the fucker calling me your daddy. What did you expect from me, to let it slide?"

"No, of course not, but that's not the point, Grady," I said as I slammed food away in the cupboards and fridge with force. "Yes, he pissed you off, and yes, he said you looked older than me. I wouldn't care if you punched him in the face for it. What I do care about is that you got jealous over the little—yes, younger than you—prick enough to take it out on me in front of said little prick and other people. I don't throw your past in your face, so I'd appreciate it if you didn't do it to me. Ever. If you're jealous, use it in another way. Show them that you have me. Show them I'm *yours* now. Mark your territory. Show them why I'm with you."

I sighed and faced him where he stood, leaning against the kitchen bench with his arms crossed over his chest and a scowl on his face. "You know that no matter what anyone says about our age, I just don't give a fuck, right?'

He grunted.

"Jesus, Grady. Don't let this get to you. You're the one I want…" I gulped and laid it out there, "…the only one I'll *ever* need."

His eyes flashed something, but I couldn't see what it

was, because in the next second, I was in his arms and his mouth was assaulting mine.

And I loved it.

He pulled back and said, "Next time some punk gives us shit, I will take you right in front of 'em to show that you are mine."

I rolled my eyes and giggled like a schoolgirl. "Sure, handsome. Now let's have sex before we go and get Swan."

He threw me over his shoulder and made a dash for the stairs.

Deanna

Three weeks later

It was bound to happen. We'd been going great after our last fight—one that could have been prevented if Grady hadn't been a jealous fuck.

Only this time, I knew it was my fault for the fight that was gonna brew as soon as he walked in the door. I'd done something I shouldn't have, and I knew it, but it was something I had to do because I had been worried. Swan wasn't up-to-speed of what a two-year-old should have been, so I took her to see a paediatric specialist. I came away with great news, but—and that's a huge fuckin' but—I shouldn't have done it without telling Grady about it first. I knew it, but still, I went ahead and did it.

And now, I was going to suffer from what would come from it.

I could only hope I wouldn't lose them in the process.

I was sitting at the kitchen table with a cup of coffee when I heard the front door open. Swan was out with Nancy, Zara's mum. I felt she and Zara were the only ones I could confide in. Both of them told me I needed to tell Grady, get it out in the open, and they were right. I'd been sitting on it for a week, and it was eating at me like a living thing.

The front door opened, and his heavy footsteps paused. I knew what he was thinking—the house was too quiet. Usually, he'd walk in and find Swan sitting in front of the television while I was getting dinner ready. Instead, the only light on was the one in the kitchen, where I was waiting for my doom.

Fuck. My heart rate sped as he called out my name, a dot of worry in his tone.

"In the kitchen," I answered.

His keys hit the stand just beside the front door, and he made his way in. He stopped just inside the archway. "What's wrong? Where's Swan?"

"She's fine." I tried for a smile, but it slipped from my face as quickly as it appeared. "Ah, she's out with Nancy for a bit. I need to talk to you."

His body was tense; I could see it in his furrowed brows, clenched jaw and tight muscles under his white tee, club vest, jeans and his usual biker boots. He pulled out the chair next to me and sat down.

"I'm fuckin' stressing here, princess. What's going on?"

"I've done something I shouldn't have." I nodded to myself, looking down at my nervously wringing fingers in my lap.

"You slept around on me?" he growled.

Glaring, I snapped, "No, dickhead. Oh, my fucking God, why in the hell would you think that? I'd never, *ever* do that."

"Shit, sorry, okay. Look, I've seen you stressed, but this—what I'm seeing in front of me—is a state worse than I've ever seen you in. So please, just tell me what the hell is going on."

It was true. I knew I was showing how scared I was. I even felt sick to the stomach. I didn't want—no, *couldn't* lose them.

Ever.

"Sorry." I took a deep breath and went on. "I took Swan to see a specialist, because I was worried she wasn't developing the way normal two-year-olds do. I know I should have told you, but I was worried you'd say no. But the good news is that she's going to be fine. Yes, she's a little behind and still very quiet, but she isn't missing anything. She's a bright young girl, and with our help, she'll be up to the standard soon." I looked up from the table. The first thing I saw was that his fists were clenched on the table in front of him, and as he leaned forward on his elbows, he brought his angry face in front of mine.

"Who in the fuck do you think you are? She is *my* girl, *my* daughter, and what she does has nothing to do with you. I would have done it. I was getting there, but then you just had to go and prove to everyone I'm a shit father to my own baby girl."

Tears filled my eyes. "No one knows," I uttered.

He shoved the chair back with a foot and stepped away from the table.

"Bullshit. You wouldn't have kept your big trap shut. Fuck. You need to stay outta my business, and that means my daughter. Not yours. Do you damned well get that?"

I knew it would be bad…just not *this* bad.

Standing, I gripped my own fist to control myself,

because I so wanted to punch him and wail like a little baby, all at the same time.

"All right, Griz." His head moved back, his eyes widening at the way my voice was…sad, and because I'd called him Griz. "I'm so fuckin' sorry I involved myself in *your* business." *You fuckin' arse.* Couldn't he see he was doing the same goddamn thing by moving in here in the first place? *The two-faced fucker.* "It won't happen again," I said and left the room.

"Where are you goin'?" Grady yelled. He stomped after me.

I picked up my bag and keys near the front door and looked over my shoulder. "I think you need time away from me. I'm going out for a while." I opened the front door.

"I don't fuckin' think so. You're staying; we need to talk."

"Don't you mean you need to yell at me more? I'm not staying for that." I took a breath and faced him. "In my heart, Grady…" I tapped my chest "…in my heart—the one you and *your* little girl made whole—I was trying to do what's best. I can see I was wrong and I'm sorry for it…no, fuck that. I'm *not* sorry. Now I know what I have to do to help Swan." I laughed sadly. "Oh, wait, now I know what *you* have to do to help Swan. I'll be sure to let you know.

You're a great father, Grady. I've never said any different to anyone. I just wanted to help...isn't that what families are supposed to do?"

Spinning back around, I quickly made my exit, shutting the front door behind me before he could say anything else. I was in my car and pulled onto the road before the dam broke.

Sniffing and wiping my nose, I pulled over and grabbed my phone. She answered after two rings.

"Hey, hun. What's happening?" Zara asked.

I bit my lip and took in a deep shaky breath.

"Deanna?" She sounded panicked now.

"I-I...can we talk? Can I come get you?"

"Sure, yes. Drive safe and come get me."

"See you soon," I whispered. I hung up, only to dial a different number.

"Satan girl, how are you doing, my lovely?" Julian answered.

"A-are you up for a girls' night?"

There was a pause on the other end. "You okay, sweetie?"

"No," I answered honestly.

"I didn't think so, and you know I'm always up for a girls' night. Do you want me to meet you somewhere?"

Blinking hard to fight the tears, I said, "I'll come get you. I just have to pick up Zara first."

"Okay, I'll be ready. What are you wearing?"

Looking down at myself, I realised I was only in jeans and a tee. That wouldn't matter though; I wanted to go somewhere quiet.

"Jeans and a tee, why?"

"So I know what to dress in. I don't think boxers would go over really well, and doll, I have to look better than you—can't have all the guys spying on your lush form."

I snorted a laugh. "Th-thanks, Julian. I needed that."

"I know, biscuit. I'll see you soon."

Griz

Fuck, shit. What had I done? Yeah, I was pissed, but I was more pissed at myself for behaving the way I did. I raised my goddamn voice at her and told her to mind her own business.

Dammit.

This *was* her business. Swan and I were hers.

She was right; this *was* what families did for each other, and I knew—once I had calmed down—all she was trying to do was help.

Still, at that moment, I'd seen red, which I fuckin' regretted it in a huge way.

She wasn't like Kathy; she wasn't like the other gold-digging, controlling bitches I'd had in the past. No, Deanna was different, and yet here I was, treating her like she was the same as those other hoes.

Motherfucker. I was the biggest idiot in the whole world.

As I sat on the couch with my head in my hands, thinking about how I was gonna save this, the front door opened. I was off that couch in seconds, but when the door came further open and in walked Nancy with a sleeping Swan in her arms, I growled and then sighed. My shoulders slumped as I walked up to them to grab Swan from Nancy without saying a word.

"What did you do?" Nancy glared and spun Swan away from me. "No, wait, don't tell me just yet. I want to tell you off good and proper without a child in my arms. I'll go put her to bed. You go and make me a cup of tea." Without an answer from me—not that I could have fuckin' given her one, since I was gob-smacked she'd spoken to me that way; I was fuckin' forty for God's sake—Nancy moved from the room to the hall, and then I heard her footsteps on the stairs as I made my way into the kitchen.

I was leaning against the bench with a cup in my hand and staring at the floor when I heard Nancy approach the kitchen.

"How'd you know I'd done something?" I asked as I looked up to see her walking to the other side of the bench.

"Pfft, please. I know a wounded, this-is-all-my-fault look from a mile away. Richard has them all the time."

Setting the cup of tea in front of her when she sat in a chair at the bench, I asked, "I guess you know what she did?"

"Yes, and...?"

"She should have come to me first. I should have taken Swan, not her."

"Don't give me that shit, young man," she snapped and sat her drink back down in front of her once again. Fuck, from her glare I could tell I was in for a lecture—one that I was too old for, but probably deserved.

"Tell me, Grady. Who was it that moved himself into Deanna's house? Who was it that had forced himself *and* his child onto Deanna without taking in any of her feelings?"

"It's not like she argued about it," I replied pettily.

She scoffed. "Of course she didn't. She knows who she has to deal with when it comes to you alpha males in the biker club. She knew she didn't have a chance. But it wasn't that. She knew not to fight, because this—you and Swan—is what she wanted. She's had you living here for some time now, and she has adapted to become a part of that little girl's life up there." She pointed to the ceiling, indicating Swan's room above us. "Still, anyone could tell it worried her that she was going to be a bad influence on Swan. But it was *you* who showed her she was more than just a loud-mouthed young lady. You let her in also, Grady Daniels. So, of course she's going to open her heart and soul to not only you, but that precious baby, and do things for you both—sometimes without thinking, but she does it because she cares so much for you both. But now you've thrown some of it back in her face…haven't you?"

I looked away. Fuck. I had, and I'd done a lot more. I'd shoved her out of what we had—our family.

"I know I was wrong, and I can only fuckin' hope she'll forgive me for it."

Nancy cleared her throat, and when I looked over at her, she smiled. "Of course she will." She laughed. "It may take some time…and begging, but she'll forgive you. You may just need to use that nice body of yours. Seduce her." I choked and spat what coffee I had in my mouth out onto the floor.

"Ah, okay. Thanks, Nancy."

"My pleasure, dear. Oh, and speaking of pleasure, I must get home to my Richard. Thanks for the cup of tea, and be a good boy."

I was forty-years-old, and I was going red from embarrassment. How in the hell had Wildcat survived growing up with her and not turned out strange? Although, Wildcat did have her moments.

Deanna

I picked up Zara, who waddled out to the car with Talon following her. Blue and Stoke were standing out on the front porch looking on as the boss-man threatened me if I didn't bring his woman home safely. Though, his threat was a mild one to what I'd seen in the past, because once he saw my tear-stained face, he knew something big had gone down and I needed my girl.

We drove on silently and picked up Julian. I'd asked Mattie to come, but he was already in bed asleep; he hadn't been feeling well. Julian got in the car, looked at me and then Zara, and then back to me and asked, "Who do I have to hurt? I've never seen our girl like this—well, besides…nope, not even then."

I snorted.

"I know. It's even worse than when we found her with a department store in her house. Tonight, she let Talon rip her a new one—though he did it gently—and usually she'd bite back big…but nothing, and she hasn't spoken, like, at all. I think she'd dead."

Biting my lips, I mumbled, "No, but I do feel like it. And stop talking like I'm not in the fuckin' car."

"There she is." Zara smiled as she grabbed my hand. "What's the plan?"

"To talk about my feelings and shit," I said with a snarl. I hated this crap, but I needed advice. Even if he didn't like me talking—no, *opening my big trap and telling people*— he could go and get fucked by a donkey.

"Don't worry, pumpkin. We'll get you so drunk you won't even know your name."

"Sounds like a plan." I started the car and drove to the nearest pub, which was two blocks away.

Zara and Julian chatted while I consumed five shots and two rum and cokes. I was on my third when it went down the wrong way and I started coughing.

"Maybe you need to burp her; get you some practice till the peanuts are out of you."

Turning my head, I saw Zara shrug and move her arm to my back. "If you try it, I'll post that picture you took when you were drunk and running around naked out in the backyard."

She glared, uttered 'Bitch' and placed her hand back on the table. I had to laugh; her belly was just touching the table in the booth we'd sat in. Looking around the small, somewhat-clean pub, I found I liked it. It was loud and bustling with people. The jukebox was playing softly, there were two other guys at the bar and Blue was sitting in a booth three down from us. Apparently, Talon didn't trust me all that much with his wife...or had it been Grady? If it was, did that mean he still cared?

I looked back at Zara, who sat next to me, and then to Julian, who sat across from us. They were the *bestest* friends anyone could have.

Okay, I may have been a bit drunk. It sure would have explained why I burst out with, "I fuckin' love you two. I really do. I know I can be the biggest bitch, but you guys put up with me and I really appreciate it." I sighed and leaned my head against the table.

"Um, hun, you could catch something from doing that," Zara said.

"Why do I have the song, 'Ding dong the witch is dead. Which old witch? The wicked witch,' playing around in my head when I see her like this?" Julian asked.

"Screw you." I laughed and sat back up. "My life ended tonight. I told Grady about takin' Swan to see a specialist behind his back and he went ballistic. I've never seen him that mad, guys, and it was all because of me and my stupid, interfering, big trap. He hates me. He really does. He's gonna move out now," I whispered, and tears slipped outta my eyes and down my cheeks. "He's gonna move out and take that gorgeous little girl with him. Then I will have nothing." I took a breath and sighed. "Jason may as well come and kill me."

"Don't you dare say that, bitch," Zara hissed. "He was just in the moment. I'm sure he's gotten over it and feels really sorry for the way he's spoken to you, hun. I'm sure of it. Men talk and rant before even thinking about the situation."

"That they do. I know; I'm one of them...well, sort of. But Mattie does it all the time. One second he's yelling at me for something, and then later, he sees I was right all along, because I am. Then he apologizes and we have make-up sex. You just watch—you'll get home later and he'll be all sorry, and the sex will be crazy mad." He leaned over the table. "And I wanna hear about it all tomorrow. Don't even think about leaving anything out."

"He's right," Zara started.

"See? Always right." Julian smiled and winked. I snorted.

Zara rolled her eyes. "Well, this time he is. He'll be begging for your forgiveness, and then you will do the deed in the hottest way yet, and then, yes, I also want to hear all about it. I'm not getting enough; Talon's scared he'll do damage to the babies with his 'ginormous'—his words, not mine—'perfect pecker'. I'll never live that saying down." She sighed, but grinned.

"You really think so?" I asked.

"Yes," they both replied.

"Come on, cupcake from hell. I'll drive you both home and you'll see that tomorrow will be a brighter day." Julian clapped.

I hoped to fuck so.

Chapter 21

Griz

I don't know how long I'd been sitting at the kitchen table after Nancy had left, but I'd keep sitting and waiting for my woman until she was home so I could crawl up her arse and tell her how sorry I was. The phone rang, and my heart jumped into my throat as panic settled in. Had something happened? A car accident?

I reached to the phone on the table. "Deanna?" I answered.

"What in the fuck did you do to her?" Talon growled down the line.

Shit.

Ignoring his question, I asked, "Where is she?"

"Probably out drinkin' her sorrows away with Zara. Again, brother, what did you do? I've never seen her look so…fuckin' defeated. Like her world had ended. Not even when she'd told us the story about her past. Fuck, man, I'm seriously thinkin' I need to come over there and beat the livin' shit outta you for putting that look on her face."

Sighing, I rubbed at my temple with my free hand. "Maybe you should. Jesus, Talon, I really fucked things up." I sighed. "Still, I did get a stern talking-to from Nancy when she dropped Swan off. Then she proceeded to tell me she was going home to pleasure her husband."

Talon's loud laughter filled the phone. "Goddamn, brother. I seriously don't know about that woman's sanity sometimes."

"I know what you mean."

Talon's voice was back to the gruff, harder tone when he said, "So, what in the hell are you gonna do to fix this?"

"Christ, anything at all. Anything."

"Good luck with that. And if my woman comes home pissed because of you, I'll fuckin' kill you."

"Sure, but I guess I'll be dead soon anyway when Deanna gets her fight back in her." I heard a click at the front door. "I've gotta go. Talk soon." I didn't wait for a reply; I hung up the phone and listened closely to hear

Deanna come inside.

What was takin' her so long? Instead of waiting, I went to the front door and opened it. Deanna was standing there with a tear-stained face and worried eyes.

"Sorry if I woke you," she said and brushed past me, heading for the stairs.

"Darlin', we need to talk."

"I smell like smoke and booze, Grady. I need a shower," she said over her shoulder and continued on upstairs.

Fuck.

I hated seeing her like this. Where was her fight? Why wasn't she yelling in my face, calling me every name under the sun?

Making sure the house was locked up, I made my way upstairs. I could hear the shower running from the en-suite in our room. I quickly checked on Swan; she was sound asleep. I pulled her blanket up over her more, and gently rubbed her beautiful blonde hair out of her face.

"I'll make this better, baby girl," I said quietly.

Leaving her room, I made my way down the hall and walked into our room, shutting the door behind me. I pulled my tee over my head, and took off my jeans and boxers. The bathroom was misty when I entered, some of it slipping out the open door. I opened the door to the shower and stepped inside. Before she could say anything, I wrapped my arms around her waist and brought her naked, smooth, wet back against my chest and out of the hot spray of the water.

"I'm sorry, darlin', so fuckin' sorry. I shouldn't have reacted like that."

"S'okay," she uttered. "I shouldn't have done it."

"Don't. You had every right. Fuck, princess, I was pissed, because I should have been the one to do it. I should have made it a priority, but I didn't, and I was—I don't know—jealous in a way. I never should have spoken to you like that, and you should have told me so. Turn around and hit me, swear at me, anything, and everything—just so I know we're okay. I need us to be okay, darlin'." I kissed her neck. "I love that you did this for us, for Swan, for *our* family, and I'll never do or say anything otherwise ever again. Swan is as much yours as she is mine. I knew this when I went off, but I couldn't stop myself. I'm an arse, princess."

She sniffed. *Damn, is she crying?*

"You *are* an arse." She shifted in my arms and turned to face me. "It's why I walked away. I knew you needed time to get your anger under control, and I was proven to be right." She smiled. "But, Grady, if you ever fucking speak to me like that again, I will castrate you." One of her hands wound around my cock and balls, squeezing hard, drawing a gasp from my mouth.

"Fuck, darlin'." I closed my eyes, only to open them seconds later. "Does this mean you forgive me?"

"For now." She smiled, got up on her toes and kissed me. Her tongue slipping over my bottom lip, I opened and our kiss deepened. My hands ran over her amazing body. I moved my mouth from hers and kissed down her neck, surprised to find her breath already heavy. I made my way with my mouth down to her left nipple, sucked it in between my lips and gently bit. She gripped my hair and the base of my neck. It was painful, but goddamn enjoyable.

After paying attention to her left breast, I moved to the right, causing a moan to fall from her lips.

Damn, my woman was hot. I gripped my dick in one hand and started to stroke, while the other hand slid between her thighs, fondling her trimmed, course hair there. She spread her legs wider and I slipped two fingers in; she was wet and ready.

"Grady," she hissed as my finger fucked her in and out. "Grady, I want you. Please."

I took a step back, my hand still around my dick, and I continued rubbing it up and down its length. She licked her lips as she watched me. A growl left my throat from the look in her eyes. She fuckin' loved to watch me, and I loved to please her.

"Darlin', I'm so damn hard for you."

"Yeah?" She smirked.

"Yes."

"I want you to fuck me, Grady. Now." She glared.

"Anything…God, fuckin' anything for you." Letting go of my dick, I gripped her wrist and pulled her against me, claiming her mouth with mine. She held me tightly, her hand fisting my hair as both my hands went to the backs of her thighs and I lifted. She wrapped her legs around me and continued our kiss.

Turning, I put her back to the wall. She gasped around my mouth from the cold, but as soon as I reached between us and placed my cock at her entrance, she moaned and then cried out when I slammed into her willing pussy.

She tore her mouth from mine, her head falling back against the tiles.

"Grady, God, yes! That feels so good."

"Damn, darlin'," I growled as my cock drove in and out of her hard and fast. This was what we needed—to dominate one another, to let our bodies say this was how it was supposed to be.

I was so fuckin' happy she'd forgiven me, and all I could do was show her my appreciation with my words and body. She drove me crazy, but I fuckin' loved it.

Her head fell to my shoulder, her arms encircling my neck more tightly and she hissed out, "Fuck, you make me feel so good, you arse."

I chuckled. "That I am, but one who will always fight for your forgiveness."

"Oh, Grady…just don't piss me off; though this was worth it…oh, God," she groaned as I shifted and tilted myself up more to touch that sweet spot inside of her.

"Yes, babe, right there."

"Darlin', hell, I'm gonna come soon."

"Me too. Keep going, please…d-don't stop. Yes!"

Two pumps later, she was gone, crying out and raking her nails down my back. A loud groan fell from my mouth as I released my seed inside of her.

"Wow," she mumbled against my neck.

"You got that right." I smiled and kissed her temple. "Maybe I should yell at you more often."

"Don't even fuckin' think about it." She pinched my back.

"I hope when I say never I can mean it," I said as I slip out of her, making sure she was steady on her feet. "But I know I can be bad-tempered. Just remember, I'll always be sorry, and eventually, I'll tell you that, once I've cooled down."

"I know, babe. It's why I'll keep you around a bit longer."

I grinned down at her and wondered if it was too soon to talk about babies.

Shit, where in the hell did that thought come from? I was a bloke, for God's sake—a guy doesn't think about kids before the chick does.

Christ! I was a fuckin' goner for this woman.

Griz

Two Months Later

I was sitting in Talon's office with him, Blue and Stoke just shooting the shit, but I could not stop fuckin' smiling, because I kept thinkin' about the way Dee had woke me up that morning.

Before I even had my eyes open, my dick was in her mouth, her hand was between her legs and she masturbated as she blew me, and what a fuckin' perfect sight to wake up to.

The thought of staying in bed all day with her crossed

my mind many times, just like it had in the last two months we'd spent together. We now moved in a certain, day-by-day routine. The days she worked, Swan was at Wildcat's; the days she didn't, she offered to have Swan with her. Not only did Swan love it, but so did Deanna. I felt like such a cock over how I reacted to Deanna taking her to see someone. I'll regret my reaction and the pain I saw in her eyes every fuckin' day. I was still grateful she forgave me and we'd moved passed it. I'd do my best to make sure I'd never do that to her again.

It was beautiful seeing her with Swan, with *our* baby girl.

One night, I was nearly brought to my knees when Swan came up to me as I was sitting on the couch watching a football game on TV. She hopped up on my knee, looked up to my face and started singing the alphabet song. As she continued, my eyes and mouth grew wider and wider.

Once she'd finished, I heard clapping from the kitchen doorway and found Deanna with a proud smile upon her face. She bounded over to Swan, picked her up in her arms and spun her around, telling her how perfect she was.

My chest ached, and for the first fuckin' time in my life, I had tears welling in my eyes.

Fuck, I was a man for God's sake. I was not supposed

to feel shit, and if I did, I wasn't supposed to show it.

From that day on, Swan bloomed into a beautiful, chatty young girl, and I had no other person to thank but Deanna. My woman.

And believe me, I thanked her every night. I could not get enough of her sweet, tight pussy, and she knew it and loved it.

"Griz?" Talon's bark brought me back to the room.

"What?" I answered with a slight jump.

They all laughed.

"Your mind seems to be elsewhere; should we take this meetin' up another day?" Talon asked.

"Nah, it's cool."

"You sure about that, brother?" Blue queried and looked down at my crotch.

What. The. Fuck?

I glanced down to see I had a boner. A fuckin' boner in a fuckin' meeting.

Shit.

"Ha! The fucker's blushin'," Stoke teased.

"Screw you," I growled.

"Well, if that's what you were thinkin' about to get hard—"

"Do not finish whatever you're about to say, dickhead,"

I warned.

They all chuckled.

"All right, settle. Let's get back on track," Talon said, just as the office door opened and Pick stuck his head in.

"You needed to see me, boss?" he asked Talon.

"Get your arse in here," Talon ordered.

I noticed Pick paled. I couldn't blame the guy. Ever since he got outta the hospital after being shot, he'd been weary of not only Talon, but all the other brothers.

He had every right to be. No one looked at, treated or spoke to him the same, all because he was stupid enough to betray the brotherhood.

Damn well lucky Talon was married to Wildcat, and Pick was the one to save her brother and his lover's lives that night, or else he would've been a dead man also. Just like Wildcat's ex.

But no, instead, he was still in the brotherhood and still fuckin' living...only on a tighter rope.

"Pick, any news on that wanker Ryan?"

He stepped into the room, but came no further. He swallowed and said, "No. Killer and I watched him pack up two months ago and drive outta town, down toward Geelong Way. I've kept an eye on him myself, but he hasn't done shit. Just sitting low in a fuckin' huge-ass house on the beach."

"Anyone come and see him?" I asked.

Pick turned to me and nodded. "Yeah, one time. Maxwell. It was about a month ago. He was all bandaged up still from our visit. He went in, stayed an hour and then left again. Other than that, nothing."

"Maybe we should have closer eyes on him," Blue suggested.

"Whadya mean?" Stoke asked.

"Have Warden, Vi's worker, get in and set some cameras up."

"Not a bad idea. Get on that," Talon said to Blue, who nodded in return.

"Still can't believe that monster of a man can sneak into any place undetected."

"I didn't either until I saw it myself," Talon said. His brows furrowed, obviously remembering that day—the day he nearly lost his woman.

"What about Maxwell?" I asked.

"Would he really be stupid enough to do anything?" Pick asked.

I looked from Talon, to Blue, to Stoke. "Yes," we all said in unison.

"All right, inside-eyes on him as well. I know we got

others on him day and night, but I'd feel a lot fuckin' better if we had eyes on him at all times. What would be even better is if either of them would make a goddamn move already. I hate this waiting shit," Talon said, and everyone nodded.

"We still got his phone tapped?" I asked.

"Yeah," Stoke replied, "but that's also givin' us shit all."

"Okay, let's get to doin' the crap we need to," Talon barked. Everyone but the two of us disappeared from the room. Blue was the last to leave, closing the door behind him.

"How's business?" I asked.

"Pickin' up every fuckin' day, so it's good, but you didn't stay around to ask that. What's up, brother?" he asked, leaning back in his chair and crossing his arms over his chest.

"You're right, but it ain't nothing. I gotta go fix that Harley that was brought in yesterday. Catch'ya later."

I went to stand until Talon growled, "Sit the fuck down."

With a grumble, I complied. "What?" I asked.

"If you don't tell me what's on your goddamn mind, I'll spread the word about your boner to everyone."

"Fuck you. Besides, not like Blue hasn't already told

everyone already."

Talon chuckled. "True that."

I shifted my weight in the hard seat, contemplating if I was really gonna tell Talon.

"Brother, just spill it."

"Fuck, I feel like a little girl talkin' about this shit."

Talon's eyes widened. "You askin' Hell Mouth to marry you?"

"How? What? Fuck. Yes."

Talon's wild, wide smile was catching.

"Shit, Griz. I knew it right from the start. The way she watched you, and the way your eyes followed her every fuckin' move, I *knew* this day would come. And I couldn't be more damned happy for you."

"Fuck." I grinned and looked down at my boots. "Thanks, brother."

"When's he gettin' out?" he asked, obviously changing the subject so I could stop feeling like a pussy.

I growled, "In a month."

"We'll up the security then. We'll get the bitch before he even breathes her air."

I looked up at him and knew my eyes were hard. "Yeah, we will."

Talon chuckled, and I looked at him with a questionable

gaze. This wasn't a laughing matter.

"Damn smart move, though," he said.

"What?"

"Moving in with her before her shit actually started. It gave you both time to get to know one another."

I laughed. "It was more than smart; it was fuckin' brilliant."

Deanna

It was Sunday morning; Grady had gone to the compound for a meeting, and I'd organized to meet up with Zara and the monsters at a play centre with Swan.

Walking in, I spotted Zara...I mean, who wouldn't? She looked like she was about to burst out the little devils any second; she was that large. Not that I'd tell her—she'd either start crying like a fool, or she'd kick my arse.

I looked to the person next to her and smiled; I should have known she'd bring her posse—Julian, Mattie, Nancy and Josie.

"Well, have a look at this proud mamma bear," Julian grinned. I made sure none of the kids were watching and gave him the middle finger.

"Ooooh, and she's temperamental like a bear too. Must run in the family—seems her man is the big tough Grizzly."

"Cut it out, Julian," Nancy scolded. I smiled as he rolled his eyes. As I placed Swan on her feet, Nancy bent to her level and said, "Hello, sweet Swan, Maya and Cody are out there playing somewhere. You wanna come find them with me?"

Swan looked up at me. I smiled and nodded. "Hang on, squirt. You have to take your shoes off." I sat her on the chair and undid her runners. As soon as they left her feet, she jumped up and ran on with Nancy following.

"Hey, Mattie and Josie." I waved as I sat next to Zara at the long table. "And how's the whale today?" I asked her.

"I swear, if there were no kids around, I would," she picked up her bottle of water, "stick this up your arse and sit you back down."

We all burst out laughing.

"Isn't it funny how they've changed roles? Deanna's now the non-swearing, calm, nice one, and Zara's turned into hell on wheels," Mattie stated.

"It's amazing what children can do for you," Nancy said as she sat back down next to me. "Josie, you should block your ears around Zara now. She's been so vile lately."

I watched Josie giggle into her hand. "I think it's

funny," she said.

"Deanna," Nancy started; I looked around Zara, "I just wanted to say, sweetheart, that I'm very proud of you." *Oh, shit. Shit, no. I cannot take this.* "I've known you for some time now, even before Zara went through that terrible business. When I met you over Skype, I knew you'd be a true, trustworthy friend for my baby girl, but I also knew from your foul-mouthed attitude you had your own stuff to deal with. I know you still are, but the way you've grown these last months is amazing. I am very proud, and I'm positive you have a great thing going with that hunk of a man of yours and beautiful girl over there." I turned my wet eyes to see Swan sitting in a ball pit with Maya and Cody, laughing and smiling.

"Thank you," I uttered. Zara placed her hand over mine on my thigh and gave it a squeeze.

"Mum, enough of the sweet words. My emotions can't take it," Zara said.

"Oh, shhh."

"Now, if I wasn't taken, I'd be all over that," Julian piped in, lifting his eyebrow in the direction of the entrance. We looked toward the door to see Pick walking in. I turned back to the other side of the table in time to see Josie blush and look down to her lap.

Hmm, what was going on there? I had thought she was still infatuated with Billy.

Zara stood up and asked, "Is everything all right, Pick?"

"Yeah, Wildcat, sorry if I scared you. Talon just wanted me to hang for a bit. I…ah, didn't want to do it outside, in case someone got the wrong impression seeing a biker sit out the front of a play centre full of kids."

She smiled at him. "That's fine. Take a seat."

"On my lap," Julian said. Mattie hit him in the shoulder as Pick rolled his eyes and chuckled. He chose to sit at the end of the table next to Josie, on a chair, of course, but backwards. "What?" Julian asked Mattie. "I was just offering." He grinned, and then said under his breath, "Like you weren't thinking it."

I think ever since the day Pick had saved them, they both had a soft spot for him, and it was that soft spot that kept him alive.

Holy shit.

As Nancy started complaining about the prices of food, I noticed the small, but intense look that Pick was giving…*Mattie?* What was that about?

Oh, no. Fuck. Please do not tell me Mattie was cheating on Julian. Please. I loved them both; they had to stay together.

I felt sick all of a sudden.

Mattie looked over to me and I glared. His eyes widened and shook his head, and he moved to pull out the chair next to me.

"Deanna," Zara snapped, and I turned to face her "I need food. Feed me, please."

I forced a smile and said, "You're effing lucky you're preggo."

She grinned. "Oh, I know."

I stood. "Would anyone else like anything?" After they gave me their orders, I stepped away from the table.

"I'll help you," Mattie said.

Of course you would, you cheating, lying, little fucker, who I was gonna kick the living shit out of.

We stepped up to the long line and waited.

"Will you stop glaring at me?" Mattie sighed.

I hadn't realised I was, but now that he said it, I felt my brows were furrowed and my eyes were squinty.

"Give me a fuckin' good reason why."

"Well, at least I know if you're pissed enough, you go back to swearing." He laughed.

"This is no laughing matter, cocksucker. What in the hell, Mattie? You make me want to feel like crying, and you know I hate to cry and feel shit."

We stepped forward before he said anything. "I know. Damn, I know. Look, can you just believe it isn't anything and leave it alone?"

"No."

He sighed and looked to the floor. "Deanna, you should know I would never jeopardise my relationship with Julian. I love that man with my whole heart and soul."

"Mattie, I know, which is why I don't get what that look was about, but I know it was intense enough for me to doubt that love you have for your man," I explained.

He shook his head. "What I'm about to say cannot be passed on to anyone. And I mean *anyone*, Deanna, not even Griz."

Shit. That was hard, but I had to know if I still had to beat the hell outta him.

"Okay." I nodded.

Mattie pulled me out of the line and pointed over to the toy machines. He was putting on a show for anyone who was looking our way.

"We better make this quick before Preggo-zilla comes ballin' us over, hunting for food," I said.

He smiled. "That's true." We stood in front of the machine and I placed my gold coins in to see if I could win a stuffed toy.

"Mattie, talk," I growled.

"He's confused," he said.

"Who? Pick?"

"Yes."

"About what?"

Mattie looked at me; I looked back. "Oh," I said.

"I think it has something to do with the fact that Julian and I helped him through…everything. He knows he'd be a dead man if I wasn't the brother of his boss's woman."

"Oh," I said again.

"He thinks he likes me, but he also thinks he likes Josie. You know how Ma is; she knows we were helping him, and in return, she thinks she's helping him by inviting him over for dinner. Sometimes I'm there, sometime not, and he gets to spend time with Josie."

"Mattie," I whined.

"I know. I've told him that nothing can happen. I've also told him he only thinks he likes me because of everything that happened, but he's not sure. Ever since he's cut ties with his mum, he's leaned on not only me, but my parents as well."

"What are you going to do?" I asked.

"Nothing. There is no way I would leave the other half of me. Julian is my life. Pick knows this and accepts it; he just has trouble hiding his feelings at the moment."

"Well, this has blown me outta the water." I shook my head and sighed. "Pick thinks he's gay."

"No," Mattie said.

"What?" I gaped. More? There was fuckin' more to this?

"Apparently, he knows he's bisexual."

"How?"

"Um..."

"Mattie," I growled again.

"No, no, nothing like that. I didn't do anything."

"Then what?"

"He, um...he told me he knows, because he still loves to..." he coughed and whispered, "fuck women and...he, um...he went to a certain club and...yeah. You can just guess what happened there."

"With a man?"

"Yes."

"Oh, wow. Okay, I mean, not that anything like that bothers me. It's just...it's Pick. He's a biker. I didn't know there were bi bikers."

Mattie burst out laughing. "Honey, there's bi, gay or curious in all walks of life. Oh, look you won." He pointed at the machine and yes, I had indeed won a freaky-looking bear. Still, I knew Swan would love it.

"Deanna," Zara bellowed across the room. I shifted around to look over at her. She pointed to her belly and then her mouth. I chuckled, took the bear in one hand and Mattie's hand in my other and moved back to the line before Zara went on a killing spree.

"You won't say anything?"

I rolled my eyes at him. "Of course I won't. To anyone. I promise. I'm just happy I don't have to hurt you now."

Mattie laughed. "Yeah, me too."

Griz

Fuck, I hated Mondays. I hated leaving Swan with Wildcat while Deanna went to work. I hated leaving Dee in bed alone before she had to get up for work. At least I had the chance to wake her up early enough—before Swan was even awake—for some morning entertainment.

Shit, I really had to get my body under control.

Just thinkin' about how wet she was for me had me hard, and now wasn't the time. I bent over the hood of the Chevy to try and work out what the fuck was wrong with it.

But yet again, my mind drifted to Dee and that morning, because it had been different. Instead of fuckin', screwin' or just getting my jollies off, we'd made love. It was slow, sweet and damn unbelievable. I knew she'd felt it too; I saw it in her eyes.

She'd woken up on a moan, with my hand in her panties flicking her clit. "Griz," she'd hissed.

"Darlin', you don't call me that here in this bed while I'm playing with you."

She'd nodded before my finger took her over the edge. I'd gotten up on my knees, my hard-on pointing in the direction it wanted to go. So I pulled her panties down and off as she lay on her back and watched, with lust-filled eyes and a cute smirk on her mouth. In a quick rush, my boxers were gone and I was between her outstretched legs.

"Grady," she'd growled, because I was holding back. I had my dick just at her entrance, my arms and hands braced on the bed beside her waist. I hovered over her. She wanted me to plunge in, but I didn't. Instead, as I kept her gaze, I slowly pushed my cock inside her tight, wet pussy. She saw it then, what it was I had intended. I needed this—the slow, passionate warm-up for making love to my woman. Her eyes filled with tears, and as I withdrew from her warmth and sank back in, I bent and kissed her tears away.

"Fuck, darlin'," I growled as I got back up on my arms to watch her. "You feel so, so good."

"Grady," she moaned.

"Slow and easy, princess. Shit, this is us, darlin'. This is what we've got," I said and witnessed the warmth seep into her eyes.

She knew. She got it.

"Babe," she'd uttered and wrapped her arms around my neck, tuggin' me down on top of her. "I-I love this—us," she whispered, and then pulled me into a fierce, smouldering kiss.

My dick, still moving slowly in and out of her, knew it was only seconds away from shootin' its load. Only, there was no way I was lettin' my woman—my old lady—fall behind. I went to reach between us, but stopped when Deanna grabbed my wrist and brought it up to link our hands and fingers together.

"I'm nearly there, babe. Hell, so close, just from you— from your dick."

"Fuck," I groaned.

"Oh, damn. Grady." Her tight walls clenched around my dick, and grunted moans fell from my lips as I planted my seed inside of her.

Goddamn it. I threw the spanner down to the concrete floor and stood up straight. My mind was definitely not at work. I needed to be embedded in my woman's pussy. My dick was achin' for release, but there was no way of getting it. Deanna was at work; otherwise, I would've rode straight home and had my way with her, and she'd be more than fuckin' happy to oblige.

I looked down at my hard cock, thankin' my damn lucky stars that the garage wasn't full of other brothers. Only a few were scattered here and there, but no one who'd take notice I was palming my dick through my jeans.

Christ. I was palming my dick at work.

What the fuck had my woman done to me?

There was only one way to fix it so I could get some work done. I walked outta the garage and over to the compound.

Another blessin'—no one was around while I walked through the building and into my room. I closed and locked the door, and then leaned against it.

Shit. I can't believe I was gonna do this, like some stupid, horny kid.

With my fingers on my zipper, I pulled it down, undid the button, reached in and grabbed my hard cock. A moan slipped past my lips. I pulled my dick outta my boxers and started strokin' it as I walked over to the bed and sat down.

Up and down, my hand slipped with ease. A picture of Deanna popped into my mind, spreading her legs wide for me like our first time. I imagined her playing with Vinny, as she called her vibrator, rubbing it over and over across her clit and then down, pushing it in and out of her dripping hole.

"Shit," I groaned. With my other hand, I pulled my black tee up and over my head, leaned back on the bed on one elbow and watched as my hand moved faster and faster stroking my dick.

A picture of Deanna riding my cock was what ripped a moan from my lips and had me comin' all over my own stomach.

Fuck. I was feeling the need to stay in bed and sleep for a while after comin' so hard, but I had shit that needed to be done. So I grabbed an old tee I musta left there a while ago from the other side of the bed and cleaned myself up.

A smile etched across my face. I really needed to play out that first time with Deanna again, and even have Vinny join us. After cleaning up in the adjoining bathroom, I made my way back out.

As I was just getting through the door to the garage, Town, a younger club member with shaggy blond hair and beady eyes, stepped up to me.

"Hey, brother," he said.

"What's up, man?"

"Not much. I gotta work on a bike some bird is bringing in later. Though, I'd rather work on her, if ya know what I mean." He chuckled.

I rolled my eyes. "Yes, Town."

"Hey, do you know where Talon is?"

"I saw him this mornin'; he said he was doin' shit at home today. Why, you need him?"

"Oh, no reason. Just wanted to shoot the shit."

Like Talon would fuckin' want to. He couldn't stand this little shit, but he was good at what he did—fixin' bikes.

"So what's been happenin' with you, brother?" he asked.

"Just the usual stuff."

"Any, you know, *secret stuff* I can help out with?"

"What the fuck are you talkin' about?" I was starting to lose my good vibe after comin'.

"Oh, you know...drugs."

I got in his face and hissed, "Listen here, you little shit. You've been here five months; you should know by now we don't deal with that shit, and if you ever fuckin' try to bring it in or on our territory, which you are a goddamn part of, I'll rip shreds through you—after Talon is done with you, that is."

"Yeah, all right, brother. Cool it. I didn't mean anything

by it; I just thought all motorcycle clubs dealt with that sorta stuff. I wasn't hearing anything about it, so I just assumed I wasn't high enough in ranks to hear about it. But now I fuckin' know. Damn, you don't need to put my balls in a vice about it."

"Town, grow the fuck up."

Walking off, I looked to my side to see he was following. I stopped at the Chevy, picked up the spanner again and started to work on it.

"Soooo…"

"Town, go find somethin' to do," I growled.

"Come on. I just wanna get to know you."

Sighing, I said, "There ain't nothing to know."

"Sure there is. I heard you got yourself a sweet piece of arse, but that she can be a ball-busting bitch. At least you've got a replacement mamma for your offspring. I bet that's all you're with her for, right?"

I needed this fucker to get outta my space, or I was gonna punch the arsehole out.

Which was why I said, "Yeah, brother, that's why I put up with her; she's a nice replacement-mum for Swan."

"Oh, shit," Town laughed.

"What?" Why in the hell I was encouraging him to talk, I didn't know.

"Is your woman blonde, with a smokin' body and blue eyes?"

Standing, I moved closer. "I'm startin' to get sick of you talkin' about my woman. Like I said, grow the fuck up and you may find something special like I did. No, she ain't a replacement. She never was. I was just lucky enough she was interested in me. Now you say one more word about her, I swear you'll be breathin' by a machine."

His eye widened. "Fuck."

"What?"

"Man, don't kill me, okay? She, your woman, was just here, and she just heard your earlier replacement comment."

"*What?*" I yelled.

"Sorry, brother. She was just here, but ran when she heard that."

I pulled my fist back and clocked him in the jaw. He cried out in pain and fell to the ground.

"Never call me a brother again, and you'd better goddamn pray nothin' comes of this little fuck up."

Running to the door to hopefully catch her, I was stopped short when Zara waddled in looking angry as all shit.

"You." She pointed. She walked up to me and stabbed

me in the chest with her finger over and over again. "You wanna tell me why my best friend just left here crying?"

I grabbed her finger and said, "It was all a mistake, so don't stress before you squirt the little people out. I'll fix it. That dick," I gestured with my chin to Town, still lying on the ground with several brothers standing around him laughing, "was annoying the...I don't have time to explain. I gotta go find her. Wait, why are you here?"

"Ma came and got Swan this morning; she wanted to take her to the shops. Talon wanted me to get out of the house, so he sent me to grab some stuff from his office. He said I was driving him crazy, Griz, but all I wanted was sex. I heard it brought on labour, but he wouldn't have it. Oh, no...I mean, he had me once, but he wasn't doing me the second time." She chuckled. "Okay, we did it the second time, but—" My hand went over her mouth.

"Wildcat, I love you like a sister," I began, and tears shone in her eyes, "but I do not want to hear about my *brother* givin' it to you."

She nodded, so I let my hand fall from her mouth.

"You love me like a sister?" she cried and wrapped her arms around my waist. Well, she tried to, but her huge belly wouldn't let her. "That means so much to me, Griz."

"Wildcat," I said and patted her on the back. "as much

fun this is, I have to go find my woman and explain."

She pulled back and stepped away. "Of course. You'll need to grovel. She hates crying, so be prepared to shift mountains for her forgiveness."

"Will do…and, Wildcat? Do me a favour, besides never talking about your sex life, go and give that arsehole a piece of your mind for causing Deanna to cry."

She grinned and said, "My pleasure."

Deanna

Stupid cocksucking wanker. To think I was there, because I couldn't get him outta my mind and wanted to screw his brains out. Stupid him, and his stupid way he loved me that morning. Just thinkin' about it had me near coming on the spot.

But now all I wanted to do was rip his beautiful cock off.

I was crying once again, for God's sake. Crying! I hated it.

If it wasn't one way—where he was yelling at me to butt out—it was another—saying I was just a replacement for Swan. Maybe that was why he apologised so quickly?

It couldn't be; I was probably overreacting, and he

probably didn't mean it that way. That idiot with him probably goaded him about the whole situation.

But damn, it had hurt.

He wouldn't be far behind me.

Though, from the look on Zara's face, he could be delayed for some time after she gave him a good scolding, which she was good at. I often felt like a five-year-old when she'd do it to me.

Serves him right.

He was sure as shit gonna pay for it when he got home. For making me cry AGAIN.

Even if I was ready to cut the shithead loose after the pain that stabbed me in my chest when I heard those words fall from his mouth, I couldn't do it. I knew there had to be a reason, so I just had to sit back and wait for him to come grovelling.

Naked.

Damn, that sounded good.

I wondered what else I could make him do before I let him off the hook.

I pulled my Mustang up out the front of my house, got out, locked it and then saw that Violet fuckin' Marcus was standing on my front porch when I rounded the hood.

"What in the hell do you want?"

"Well, hello to you too, Barbie."

"Seriously, Vi, what are you doing here?" I asked as I stepped around her and slid the key in the lock.

"Why are you upset? You've been crying."

"No I haven't, and if I had, it would be none of your fucking business," I explained and turned back to her with my arms crossed over my chest. I sighed and asked again, "What are you doing here, Vi?"

"I wanted to have a chat with you."

My eyebrows shot up. She'd shocked the shit outta me enough it was a wonder my eyebrows even stayed on my face.

"What about?"

"I think its best we go inside and have a coffee for this conversation."

Shit. This sounded bad. If she was willing to come to me, be in my presence and be willing to enter my house, it had to be some bad shit.

"Fine." Turning back, I unlocked the door, opened it and entered.

Only once I was through the threshold, I was grabbed around the neck, flung sideways and held against the wall next to the front door.

With my hands holding the one hand that was around

my neck applying pressure, I watched Vi pull her gun out and around, but in the next second it was knocked out of her hand by another guy, and then he hit her. Once she was on the ground, he was on top of her, holding her hands behind her back.

The hand around my throat tightened enough to make me cough.

"Kenny, ease up a little. We can't have her dead," the tall, thin guy with dirty blond hair said from the floor as he continued to subdue a kicking Violet.

The hand around my throat eased enough for me to get a big breath in.

"Who the hell are you? Deanna, do you know them?" Violet asked with a hard tone.

I looked from the guy with long black hair and dark brown eyes in front of me, and then back to the one on the ground.

"No," I choked out.

Fuck!

Who in the hell were these guys and what were they doing at my house?

"Doesn't matter if you know us or not. Someone wants to get to know you, so you're coming with us," the guy in front of me hissed in my face. Kenny, wasn't it?

"Boss said to only grab the blonde," the one on Vi said.

"We'll have to take both. Can't have that bitch running off to tell someone."

"No," I uttered. Obviously this was my shit if they only wanted me, so I wasn't bringing anyone along for this fucked up ride. "She won't say anything. She hates me anyway. It'll be no loss to her if you take me. Alone."

"Bullshit," Kenny spat.

"Take her out the back to the van. I'll bring this one."

"Sure, Nathan."

Shit, shit, shit.

I couldn't let this happen.

Kenny's hand slid from my throat, down over my breast and gripped my wrist tightly as he pulled me forward, heading to the back of the house.

"Violet?" I asked. She'd know what to do; she had to, right? This was what she did for a living. Well, not exactly this, but...

"It'll be all right, Dee," she called.

Fuck. That really didn't ease the tension running through my body. It didn't ease the fright running through my veins.

Goddamn it.

I started digging my heels into the ground, forcing my

weight backwards.

There was no way I was going without a fight.

"Bitch, fucking move your arse."

"No." We were passing the kitchen bench where a plate was laying. I picked it up and clobbered him over the head with it.

He let out a curse, spun and backhanded me across my cheek.

Damn it all to hell; that had hurt.

I kicked out his knees, and when he went down I turned to run, only he grabbed me by an ankle and the next second, I was on the ground with his full weight over me.

"What is going on?" Nathan yelled as he walked into the kitchen with Violet in front of him. He still had her arms pinned behind her.

She smirked down at me and gave off an eye roll.

Man, I so wanted to kick the shit outta her. Punch her in the boob. Why in the fuck was she so calm?

Then it hit me.

She had a plan.

She must have one, right?

"Get her up, dipshit, and contain her."

The weight behind me left, and I was pulled off the ground and held like Nathan was holding Violet with my arms behind my back.

"Violet?" I asked again.

Kenny spat, "Shut up, slut." He leaned over my shoulder and whispered in my ear, "You'll get payback for what you just did. I'll make sure the boss will give you to me, and after I fuck you, I'll kill you."

Shit.

Whatever Violet's plan was, it had better be good, because I was sure as shit about to pee myself.

Griz

I was just out the garage doors when my phone rang. I grabbed it from my jeans pocket, flipped it open and answered with a barked, "What?"

"Get the fuck back in the garage," Talon growled.

"Brother, I have to go find my woman and make sure she ain't setting traps to kill me in my sleep."

"I need you, man. Turn your arse around and get to *my* woman. I trust no one there but you with her."

By the scared fuckin' tone in his voice, I spun and ran back into the garage.

"What in the fuck is goin' on, Talon?"

"Kitten's water just broke. I've called an ambo and I'm

on my fuckin' way, but I want someone with her, brother."

"I'm on it," I said and hung up. He needed to concentrate on getting here without any other stress to freak him out.

Rounding a corner, a blood-curling scream tore through the garage. I ran into the room to see a puddle under Wildcat as she bent over a bench, legs apart. She was braced by one hand holding her up, while the other one had Town by the balls, and from the look on his face, he was in a large amount of pain.

Stoke, Killer and Memphis all stood around her, trying to hide their smirks.

She took a deep breath in and out, and then said, "If you cocksucking men get a woman pregnant, I swear I will hunt you down and cut off your dicks."

"Wildcat?" I asked, easing up behind her.

"Griz, what the hell are you doing here? Go find Deanna and do her. Or I'll...oh, shit." She ended with a scream and leaned her head on the bench.

"Jesus, man. Please, please make her stop," Town cried as he gripped her wrist, trying to break her hold.

Fuck. What in the hell was I supposed to do?

"Wildcat, you wanna let go of the guy's nads?" I asked gently, and then moved to rub her lower back with my palm.

"Ah, Griz. Yes. Oh, damn, that feels so good," she moaned.

"Why do I feel a hard-on coming on?" Stoke laughed. "You keep moanin' like that, lady, and you'll give us all boners."

She turned her head to glare at him.

"Shut the fuck up, dickhead," Killer barked.

"Griz," Wildcat whimpered. Christ, they were close, the fuckin' contractions were coming fast.

"Wildcat, let go of his balls and I'll keep rubbin'," I said and put more pressure into the motion of my hand on her back.

Her hand dropped away, putting it on the bench with her other and Town left in two seconds flat.

"Shit a brick. Oh...Hell!" she cried.

"Breathe, woman, breathe that shit out. Do the he-he-ha breathing they teach you," Stoke said. We all looked at him, even Wildcat. "What?" he asked. "I've seen it in movies."

"Idiot," Killer uttered.

"Tool," Memphis chuckled.

"It's all right, Wildcat. Talon's on his way; he called an ambulance. They'll be here soon."

"Good," she snarled, "they need to be here when I kill

Talon for doing this to me."

"You need anything, woman?" Killer asked.

"No!" she snapped. My hand stilled on her back as I listened to hear the sirens and the pipes of a Harley coming up the road.

"Griz, if you don't start up your hand again, I'll have to hurt you, and then Deanna will be pissed at me." I quickly started rubbing again and she groaned.

Heavy footsteps pounded down the hallway; I looked over my shoulder to see Talon with a worried expression come running in, and two EMT men entered seconds after him.

"Kitten," he called.

"You!" she yelled, stood and turned to face him while holding onto her belly.

"Shit, he's a dead man," Stoke muttered.

The EMT men reached her sides, and one said, "Come on, sweetheart, let's get you to the hospital."

"You fuckin' touch her again and call her sweetheart, I'll kill you." Talon moved himself in, gave me a chin lift and I moved in on her other side, and with our help, she waddled her way out.

"Don't go all Neanderthal on me right now, Talon Marcus. Let these nice men do their jobs; you're in enough trouble."

"They can do their damn job at the hospital. Until then, I've got you," he barked.

"I don't appreciate that tone right now, Talon." She looked over her shoulder to the smirking ambo guys. "Do you have another bed for my husband? Because I'm about to beat the shit out of him." And with that, she slogged her fist into Talon's stomach.

"Hell, woman. Whad'ya do that for?"

"You and your stupid sperm! That's why. Now get me to the damn hospital." She stopped and hunched over while Talon and I held her weight, and she screamed through another contraction.

"Kitten?" Talon's tone was gentle. Once we started moving again, she looked over at him. "We'll get through this together. I hate that you're dealing with this pain on your own; I wish I could take it away, but I can't. Just think though, kitten. Once this is done, we'll have our beautiful kids with us."

Tears shone in her eyes. "We will." She smiled. "But until then, be prepared for the ultimate bitch to be here."

"I'm ready for her, baby."

"Good."

We helped her up into the back of the ambulance, and

just as I was shutting the door, Talon grinned with fuckin' joy. "Thanks, brother."

I gave him a chin lift and said, "Anytime."

"Griz?"

"Yes, Wildcat?"

"I asked Deanna to come to the birthing suite. I need my girl there. Bring her, please."

"I'll go get her."

As I watched the vehicle leave the car park, my phone rang. "Yo?"

"Griz?" A deep male voice asked.

"Yeah."

"This is Warden."

My brow furrowed. "What's up, man?" Why was this guy calling me?

"There's been a situation. Violet has set off her safety button in her pocket."

"You need help? I can't talk to Talon. He's just left with Wildcat; they're about to be parents." I smiled.

"No. I...fuck, man. She was at Deanna's when she set if off."

My body stilled, my heart stopped and by fuck, I wanted to scream at the sky.

"I'll be at the office in five," I snarled.

"See you then."

Deanna

Violet and I were thrown—literally—into the back of a black van. We could hear the door being locked behind us. I quickly tried the side door. No luck there, it was also locked tight.

I turned to see Violet sitting calmly.

"What the fuck, Vi?" I hissed.

She pulled something outta her pocket and smiled. "It's a silent alarm that sends its signal back to the office. It's also a tracking device. By now, Warden will be rounding up the troops to come find us."

"Fuck," I whispered.

My fists went to my eyes and I flopped to my back on the steel floor. Even though it hurt, a sense of solace swept over me, because I knew that Warden would call Griz.

My man would be hunting for me.

Damn, that felt good—no *great*, ...fan-fuckin'-tastic to think of.

"But just because we know the cavalry are coming doesn't mean you can cause shit. You need to keep your mouth shut and do as they say. That way, neither of us should get hurt."

I felt my cheek; I knew it was already bruising from how tender it was. "Okay," I said and sat up to face her, where she sat at the back of the van.

Violet smirked. "What? You're not going to fight me on this?"

"I don't have the energy. I've got enough shit to worry about."

"Like your foster brother?"

My eyes widened. "Who told you?"

Violet rolled her eyes. "Come on, Barbie. I knew something was up that night we were all around for dinner at my brother's house. Even though I didn't get to stay for the information, it doesn't mean I wouldn't check."

I shrugged. "So, you know. I really couldn't care."

Violet studied me. "What else was wrong when you got to your house before?"

"Nothin' you need to know about."

"Did someone ring you about Jason Drake?"

"No, why?"

"He's out, Deanna. He got out a month early; he was released yesterday."

Panic surged through me.

Shit, just what I needed.

I scoffed. "Well, aren't you just a bringer of good fuckin' news? Glad you told me now? What, did you want to see the worry, the panic in my eyes, so you can go back and tell Travis and have a good laugh about me? About how it freaks me the hell out to know the man who murdered the only parents I knew did it all because of me? Great, thank you. Fuck!" I punched the side of the van.

Oh, God. I just wanted to curl into a ball and forget everything. But I fuckin' couldn't.

"That wasn't why I came to tell you, Deanna. I wanted to warn you."

I snorted. "Yeah, okay."

She sighed. "Look, I don't give a shit if you believe me or not; at least *I* know what my intentions were. Now tell me, do you think these idiots who took us have anything to do with Jason?"

"Hell, it hadn't even crossed my mind. But honestly, no.

He'd want to do his own work. He's never trusted anyone else. This has to do with something else, Vi, and I wouldn't have a fuckin' clue what."

"Doesn't matter. We'll figure it out. If not us, the guys will."

"Where do you think they're taking us?" I asked.

"Not sure, but it's obvious it's not some place in Ballarat."

I crossed my legs and sat straighter as I watched Vi move to lean against the side of the van. "Look, I can't help but be a bitch, and I'm not sorry for it, but I am sorry for having you dragged into this. Whatever this is."

"Aw, Barbie, you do love me." Vi laughed.

"Fuck you."

"No, thanks. I get enough at home."

I cleared my throat. *Damn, was I really going to do this? Have a bloody normal conversation with my nemesis?*

"How are things with you and Travis?" *Yeah, I guess I was.*

It had to do with the fact that my emotions were fucked. They were going haywire inside of me. I was scared, angry, worried, pissed, annoyed and did I mention scared? Not only about this stuffed-up situation, but the fact that the man who would have killed me many years ago is out walking the streets.

A free fuckin' man.

It wasn't right. No man should have been released after the crime he committed, but it showed just how crazy the system was.

In my eyes, he hadn't paid enough for what he'd done. Which was why, in some ways, I did hope he came for me, so I could enforce a better punishment.

I may have failed Zara for not following through with what I wanted to do to David—at least he was dead now—but I would with Jason. He was a sick prick who needed to be eliminated.

"Are we really going to have this conversation?" Vi asked, bringing me out of my thoughts.

Shrugging, I said, "What else is there to do. I'm not gonna sit here and play truth or dare, or braid your fuckin' hair."

Violet actually laughed. I fought the smile from my lips.

"All right, things with Travis are good."

I waited for more. "What, that's it? That's all you're going to say?"

It was her turn to shrug. "What do you want me to say?"

"I don't know, but something more at least. How are you, the PI, handling that your man is the top dog in Melbourne for selling women?"

She rolled her eyes and then glared. "Nothing is sacred in our little family, is it?"

I shook my head. "No, not really."

"How about you tell me what was up your arse when you got home, and then I'll talk to you about...that."

"Deal." I smiled. I didn't care; my information wasn't juicy gossip like hers was.

Griz

Before I left the compound on my Harley, I called Killer and told him to get Stoke and Blue to meet me at Violet's office. Then I called Nancy, Wildcat's mum, who had Swan.

"Hello," she answered.

"Nancy, it's Griz. I need you to watch Swan for a while longer."

"Sure, honey, as long as you don't mind me taking her to the hospital. You know my baby girl is gonna have her babies? I'm so excited."

"Yeah, I know. Look I gotta go—"

"Griz, what's wrong?" she interrupted to ask. How in

the fuck she knew I didn't have a clue.

"Nothin' that can't be fixed."

"Do you need help?"

Damn, she'd actually brought a smile to my face when it felt like my heart had dropped into my arse and I was about to shit it out.

"No, woman, I'll deal with it," I said and slipped my leg over my Harley.

"Deal with what, young man? What is going down; is someone hurt? Griz, do not leave me worrying."

"Nance—"

"Griz, Richard here. What's going on? Why does my wife look pale all of a sudden?"

Fuck, I had no time for this.

"Richard, shit, sorry to upset your woman, but I don't know how in the hell she knew something was going down, but it is, and I gotta cut this short so I can get things done. Long story short—my woman and Talon's sister have been taken. We know where they are, so I'm going to go get them back."

"Right, son. I'll keep things here under control. You go do what you gotta, unless you need an extra pair of hands. I've still got that gun Talon gave me."

"No, I've got my brothers to help, but I really have to

head off."

"See you at the hospital to meet my grandkiddies after you get the women back."

"Richard, what's happening? You tell me right now or I'll..." I heard in the background.

"Woman, shut it and get everyone in the car. Zara's probably holding her legs together keeping those kids in, waiting for us to get there." He took a breath and then said into the phone, "Be careful, son."

"Right," I said and hung up. With a kick, my Harley roared to life. I was finally on my fuckin' way to kill whoever put his hands on my woman.

Striding into Violet's office, I found Warden and Travis, Violet's man, standing at a desk; they both looked up from the computer and gave me a chin lift.

"What's the deal?" I asked.

"The tracker hasn't stopped, so we don't know their final destination. As soon as we do, we'll be on the road," Warden said. I looked at Travis; he seemed just as strung out as I was—any fuckin' wonder. Who knew what was going on with our women? Fuck, now I knew how Talon felt when he had to sit around waiting for information about where Wildcat had been held.

It not only fuckin' hurt, but it made you even crazier as the seconds ticked by.

"What area are they at now?" I asked.

"Heading their way to Geelong."

"Christ," I hissed.

"What?" they both snapped.

"I know where they're goin'. Let's head out and I'll explain on the way."

We all jogged out, and while Travis and Warden jumped into Travis's Hummer, I went to the back of it where Blue, Stoke, Killer and Pick pulled up on their Harleys.

"What's happenin'?" Blue asked.

I ignored him and looked at Pick. "Why haven't you spoken to Warden about an inside watch at that jackass's place in Geelong?"

"I had, Griz. I swear I had. Fuck, is he saying something else? I went straight to him that day I left the meetin' and told him what we're after. He said he'd get on it. I thought he had. Hell, I haven't done anything. I swear."

"All right, calm the fuck down." I shook my head. I could understand the panic in his eyes. He knew if he betrayed us in any way, he'd be a dead man. "Looks like

Ryan wanted payback after all. That's where the women are being taken."

"Pick, you know the way?" Stoke asked.

"Yeah, yeah, I know it."

"Okay, you lead the way. Park a street away; we'll go on foot from there. You boys know the drill."

"Yeah, course, brother," Blue said. "Should we say anything to Talon?"

"No. He's gonna be busy and worried enough with Wildcat givin' birth."

"She is?" Blue grinned. "Right on."

I turned to walk off and get in the car with a no doubt impatient Warden and Travis.

"Griz," Pick called.

"What?" I prompted over my shoulder.

"Find out why Warden hasn't done the job. Please. It wasn't me stuffin' up, brother. I swear."

I shifted to look at him and gave him a chin lift.

"Rest easy, brother," Killer said to Pick.

Yeah, we all knew Pick wasn't dumb enough to try anything behind our backs. He was back in the fold of the tight arms of the brotherhood.

Deanna

"I'd overheard Griz saying he was with me only because he needed a replacement-mum for Swan."

She snorted. "And you believed that?"

"At the time, yeah. It had hurt, but then the more I thought about it, the more I realised he was probably just talkin' shit in front of his biker buddy."

"That would be more like it."

"I know, but fuck, that still stung. I mean, why in the fuck would he want me—the dirty-talkin' sailor—around his daughter."

"Um, duh. Jesus, Barbie, everyone knows your bark is bigger than your bite. Underneath all that, you're just a big softy."

"Do you want me to fuck you up?"

Vi rolled her eyes. "Whatever. It's the reason I put up with your hating attitude toward me. I know deep down you really care for me."

I coughed out, "Bullshit."

"Again, whatever." She smirked. I covered my mouth to hide my own smile.

"I guess you're not too bad," I said.

"See, all we needed was a bonding moment by getting kidnapped together for us to speak civilly to each other." She grinned.

"I still hate you though."

She laughed. "Oh, the feeling is mutual."

"Okay, enough of this gooey shit. What's the chop with you and Travis?" I asked, moving into a position of crossing my legs and leaning back on my palms.

She stretched her neck and back, and then started with, "At first, I thought I could be with him, but after one night, when we were out in Melbourne, two of his whores spotted him, and when they came over for a friendly chat...that was when I decided I couldn't deal with his business."

"Why?" I asked.

"He'd been sleeping with them, and they made sure I knew about it. He saw how uncomfortable I was, but did nothing about it. Instead, he continued laughing and flirting with them."

"Damn. What an arse," I said with disgust.

She nodded and looked to her hands in her lap. "That night, when we got back to his house in Melbourne, I left while he was in the shower."

"So how'd it get to where it's at now?"

She smiled to herself. "He became a pain in my arse. He rang, sent flowers, emailed and popped into places I was at—even when I was out on a date with Jim Binton. Do you know him?"

"No." I shook my head.

"He's a cop, and a good one, but just not a great guy to date. Anyway, we were at a restaurant talking and eating, and then in walked Travis. With a glare, he stalked right up to our table, pulled up a chair and sat down."

A laugh escaped me. "What happened next?"

She grinned and snickered. "Jim asked him if he was all right. Travis ignored him, grabbed my hand, which I tried to pull away, and then proceeded to tell me everything he loved about me, that he couldn't see his life without me in it and now that I was back in it after so many years apart, he was not willing to lose me again. He said he would do anything to keep me in his life, and then continued on to inform me, in front of a cop, he no longer dealt with hookers. He'd passed his women on to another he trusted."

"Holy shit. What'd the cop say?"

"At first, he was shocked, but then he actually laughed. He stood from the table and wished me good luck with my future and said he could not compete with him. He threatened Travis that he would be keeping an eye on him and his dealings. Also," she laughed. "He asked Travis if he'd be willing to tell him who was now in charge of his women in Melbourne. Of course, Travis didn't."

"He's lucky he didn't get his arse taken to the station for questioning."

"I think he didn't because of me. Jim had a soft spot for me, and apparently, from what he told me when he rang the next day, he could see the way I felt for Travis from the look upon my face, and there was no way he could crash my hope in the form of any legal proceedings."

"Damn," I smiled. "And I guess from then on out you two have been attached at the waist."

"You could say that, but I'm not stupid; I've kept a close eye on him, and he's kept his word. He's now just the owner of his construction company, and the women are a thing of his past."

The van came to an abrupt stop, only to start off again. I

quickly gripped the side rail, as did Vi on the opposite side. They turned sharply, the van's tires squealing on the concrete road.

"What the fuck?" one of the guys yelled the front of the van.

"Who in the fuck are they?"

Violet and I looked at each other and smiled.

The guys had come.

That was when we heard the sound of Harleys in the distance, but coming up fast.

"Shit, Christ. We got bikers coming up," Nathan yelled.

"I'll fuckin' worry about them after I lose that damn car first," Kenny barked. "What should I do? What in the hell should I do? Boss will kill us if we bring this to his doorstep." His tone was getting louder with worry.

"Fuck!" Nathan screamed.

"Either way, we're gonna end up dead," Kenny yelled the obvious.

"Slam on the brakes," Nathan growled.

"What?"

"Hit the brakes. NOW!"

I gripped harder just as Kenny pushed his foot down on the brakes. My body twisted around with the force and I wasn't able to hold on; if I had, I would have broken my wrist. I let go and went flying to the front of the van. My head collided with the back shelf.

"Deanna? Barbie, are you okay?"

I sat up slowly, my head spinning as the car came to a stop. "Was that concern in your voice, bitch?" I asked.

Violet sighed and then laughed. "Well, damn. I guess it was."

"I'm okay. It'll just be a bruise."

"Get the fuck out," we heard a vicious voice say. I pulled my aching head up to meet Vi's eyes.

"Griz," I uttered. She smiled and nodded.

Harleys came to a stop wherever we were. My heart beat with excitement from having a chance to see my man in hero-mode.

"Move it slowly, and hand the keys over," Griz growled. "Blue, hit the doors, brother."

The back doors were unlocked and then pulled open; both Vi and I blinked until our eyes got used to the shining sun.

"Is she okay?" Griz asked.

Blue looked in and smiled widely. "Hello, sweetnesses." He then yelled around the van, "Looking good as always, brother."

"Fuckin' lucky," Griz hissed.

"Violet?" Travis yelled.

"I'm fine," she called back.

And we were. We were fine now that our men were there, even though we could have kicked some arse ourselves.

"You ladies had better get your sweet booties out of there for your men to see for themselves before a blood bath hits the streets," Blue suggested.

Vi and I shared a secret smile between the two of us before making our way to our guys.

Griz

Fifteen minutes earlier

Warden had just explained from the back seat that he had been meaning to set cameras up in both Ryan and Maxwell's place, only the business had been so busy he'd been caught up in other situations. After cursing for five minutes, he said whenever we needed something again, it would be top priority. He didn't want the same mistake to happen again.

I agreed and turned around to face the front. Pick was up ahead, and my other brothers were a few car spots behind us. I was surprised the cops weren't after our arses; Travis was driving like a maniac—it was fuckin' great.

"Take the next left," Warden yelled after lookin' down at his tracking system.

"What? Why? Pick's going that way," he growled back.

"They've turned off. Turn, motherfucker, turn"

"Shit, hold the fuck on," Travis yelled. I gripped the seat and dashboard, and saw before we spun around the corner that Pick had hit his breaks.

"With your driving, we've nearly caught them," Warden said. He looked down and then up again; his hand pointed out the front windscreen. "There, that damn van. It's got the women."

A couple of cars up the road and across a lane was a black Holden van with no number plates. For some reason, it must have spotted us; it's speed picked up.

"We ready to catch them?" Travis asked.

I pulled my .44 auto-mag pistol from its holster under my club vest. "Let's do this. They're turning! They're turning!" I yelled.

"I can fucking see that," Travis growled. He took the next lane, cutting off a car who laid on its horn, and then we were around the corner in seconds. "Bloody idiots." He

11/28/2018

Item(s) Checked Out

TITLE   Climbing out : a Hawks
BARCODE   33029066112913
DUE DATE   **12-19-18**

Terminal #   218

smiled. I looked up from my gun and out the front to see the van parked at a dead end street.

We all jumped outta the car when Warden said, "Nothing around but empty industrial warehouses." He grinned.

I stalked around the front of the van with my gun pointed directly through their window and at their heads. "Get the fuck out."

The rest of our little army came around the corner on their bikes; they stopped, and were surrounding the men in a matter of seconds, all with their own guns out.

"Move it slowly, and hand the keys over," I growled. The one who had driven held the keys high. "Blue, hit the doors, brother," I ordered. Blue grabbed the keys and ran to the back of the van.

"Is she okay?" I asked.

Blue yelled around the van. "Looking good as always, brother."

"Fuckin' lucky," I hissed at the fuckheads.

"Violet?" Travis yelled.

"I'm fine," she called back.

As Travis, Stoke, Pick and I each held a gun on the two fuckers as they knelt on the ground, Killer patted them down and threw their phones, knives and handguns aside. I

waited patiently—even if I wanted to get trigger-happy—
until I could get my eyes on my woman.

My head rose as I heard movement behind the van, and
then Deanna and Violet walked around the corner of it.
"Fuck!" I snapped. My woman had a bruise shining on her
cheek and a red bump on her forehead. What did they
fuckin' do?

Stepping forward, I kicked the one who had driven in
the stomach; he bent over coughing. "Who laid their hands
on my woman?" I snarled down at them.

"Griz," Deanna called; I looked up and she was in my
arms. I stepped back with my arms around her waist, and
she wound hers around my neck. "Fuck, woman. Fuck," I
whispered.

"I'm okay. I'm fine," she uttered. She said she was
okay, but I could feel her body shaking.

I pulled back, placed my hands on each side of her face
and searched her eyes. "Who touched you, darlin'?" I
asked.

"Wait," the guy who was still kneeling—in other words,
the one who I hadn't kicked—pleaded. He went to get up,
but Killer was behind him, and with a hard hand, he thrust
him back to the road. "Wait," he said again, "we were just
doing a job. I hardly know the guy."

I shifted Deanna behind me and said, "Then which of you was it who laid a finger on my woman? Was that in the goddamn job description?"

"It wasn't me."

"Well, fuck," the guy who was still trying to breathe got back up to his knees, "Yeah, it was me. What you gonna do about it?"

Fool.

My brothers laughed behind him. Out the corner of my eye, I saw Violet step away from Travis, and Warden then walked up beside me.

"When Deanna tried to fight back—"

"Violet, no," Dee gasped behind us.

Vi turned to her. "They'd find out anyway. In this world, Deanna, in our world with *our* men, we have to do what we have to, and that's standing by them and telling them everything they need to know."

I watched my woman close her eyes and nod. Violet looked up at me and said, "He was going to ask his boss for her. He was going to rape her, and then kill her."

"Shit," Blue hissed.

"Fuckin' A," Stoke said.

"Dead man breathing." Killer grinned, and right there was the reason he was called Killer. He loved to be the one to do it, but this one was on me.

I looked down at Violet. She took a step back from the hatred in my eyes. "What about the other one?" I asked.

"I think he was just hired help. He was…nicer, gentler."

With a chin lift, I stomped back to Deanna. "Darlin'…"

"What are you going to do?" she asked.

"What I have to. No one touches what's mine; no one lays a harmful hand on my woman and still lives." I told it to her straight; now it was up to her to choose to still be with a man like me…or not. If she chose she couldn't, I'd understand; it would fuckin' kill me, but I'd understand, because I had blood on my hands from my past, and I was sure in my near future.

She studied my face and saw the truth of my words. I expected her to flinch and turn away in disgust. What I hadn't expected was her to nod and say, "You do what you have to, whatever you deem necessary."

Fuck.

I stepped close to her, and I carefully placed my hand under her chin to bring her face up as I leaned down. "You are my woman."

She grinned. "I know, and you're my man…but I can't be here for this."

"I know, and I would never expect it." My gaze

explored hers and I saw it. Fuck, did I see it. "You know I love you right? And I'd only do good by you."

Tears shone in her eyes. I knew now wasn't the time to confess my feelings—with an audience and with what I was about to do—but I couldn't hold it back. I couldn't *not* tell her.

She nodded and gave me a sweet, soft kiss. I pulled back and turned. "Pick, you need to leave your bike and take the women to the hospital."

"I don't need to go," Deanna said as she came up to my side and placed her arms around my waist. I moved to fit her as close as I could get her next to me with my arm around her shoulders.

"Just get it checked, and besides…Wildcat's waiting for you. She's popping out her kids."

"What! Shit, fuck. I need to go; she'll need me there. Pick, get your arse in that car. You too, Violet," my woman ordered. She nearly tore my head off as she pulled my head down, kissed me hard and said, "See you there?"

"Yeah, darlin'," I laughed. "We won't be long."

"Travis?" Violet called from the car.

"I'll meet you there," he said. He was coming with us.

She looked concerned, but nodded and got in the car.

I was ready to complete the next stage of my plan.

Chapter 31

Deanna

Pick got us to the hospital in under an hour. It could have had something to do with the amount of abuse spilled from my mouth if he didn't get us there on time.

I just hoped like fuck Zara held those little monsters in until I arrived.

He dropped Vi and me off at the door, and went off to park the car. We raced in and straight up to the elevators. It seemed to take forever for one to arrive on the ground floor. People who stood with us waiting, backed up a bit as I swore and cursed the slow-moving machine.

On the fifth floor, we spotted the birthing suite and saw Zara's parents waiting out the front with Josie, Mattie, Julian and the kids.

Swan popped up from the seat; as soon as our eyes met, she ran at me. I got down on one knee and braced for her lunge. Her arms wound around my neck, and she hugged me as tightly as I was her.

Tears filled my eyes. I had been so worried I'd never get to see her again.

She pulled back and touched my cheek. "Sore, Mummy."

Oh, fuck.

Oh, shit.

Goose bumps broke out all over my skin. I had heard her right, hadn't I? She'd called *me* mummy.

"It's okay, sweetheart. I'm okay," I said through a choked-up voice and tears.

She smiled and kissed my cheek gently. Nancy came up behind Swan and I looked up at her. She had her own tears shining in her eyes. "You'd better get in there, honey. She's been waiting for you."

Nodding, I looked back at Swan and said, "I'll be back out soon, okay? You stay with Nancy."

"Okay, Mummy."

Hell. That precious girl had just made my shit day so much better and brighter. Now all I needed was to have my man at my side.

God, I hoped he was okay.

As I stood, Mattie and Julian came up. "Are you good, sugarplum?" Julian asked.

"I am now." I smiled, bent over and kissed Swan on her forehead.

I walked through the doors to the front desk and asked for Zara's room. A male nurse smiled and said, "Follow me." We started off down a hallway. "You must be Deanna. She's been screaming at her husband to get you here."

I laughed. "Yeah, that's me."

He pointed. "Right in there, and good luck." He grinned as a scream came from the room I was about to enter.

"Huh, thanks." I stepped forward, took a deep breath and pushed the door open.

"I swear, Talon, I swear you're having your balls removed. I am not doing this again."

"We'll see, Kitten."

Zara was bent over the double bed, the side of her face planted into the mattress, as Talon stood to the side of her and rubbed her lower back. Another nurse, this one female and young, stood on the other side of Zara, holding a tube that was hooked up to a machine.

Talon saw me first and smiled, only it faded as he took in the bruise on my cheek and the bump on my forehead.

"What the fuck happened to you?" he growled.

I shook my head and mouthed, *I'll tell you later*. I was here for Zara, not anything else.

"What the hell do you mean? You knocked me up, dickhead!" Zara yelled.

I laughed; her head popped up and met my gaze.

"That's right, bitch. It's all your boss-man's fault."

"Deanna," she breathed. Tears overflowed from her eyes and she sniffed. "I thought you wouldn't make it," she whispered, wiped her eyes to clear the tears and glared at me. "Where have you been, wench? W-what happened to your face?"

I moved forward to lie on the bed and get close to her face. "I'll tell you all about it after you've laid your damn eggs."

"De—oh shit! Give me that machine!" she screamed, and snatched the tube from the nurse, placed it in her mouth and breathed through it over and over through her contraction.

After it passed, she threw it to the side. "Oh, man, I love that stuff." She laughed and looked at me. "You know when we got stoned that time, that," she pointed at the machine, "gives me a wicked buzz. Is my voice funny? It sounds funny."

I rolled my eyes. "No, dipshit, your voice isn't funny. Maybe Talon and I should try some of that stuff?"

"Don't you dare," she growled. "I'm still mad at the both of you—him for impregnating me, and you for being late. So you can suffer through this."

The nurse moved, put gloves on and her hand disappeared under Zara's pink nightie.

"What are you doing?" I yelled. "Don't put your hand up there when the monsters are trying to come out. Jesus." Thank fuck I missed all this shit and waited in the waiting room when she had Maya. No wonder my brain told me I'd be scared to watch this shit stuff.

"Calm down, Hell Mouth. She's just checking how far dilated she is," Talon said.

"Whatever that means. Hey, Zara?"

"What, hun?" She sounded so tired. I glanced up at Talon to see he had worry in his eyes.

"At least you can say you've had a lesbian experience now."

She chuckled and said, "Fuck you. Oh, oh. Tube me, tube me!" she yelled. I quickly passed her the sucky thingy. She latched onto it like it was Talon's dick and sucked hard.

"Not long now," the nurse said after Zara's pain had passed. "When the next contraction hits, try pushing, okay,

Zara?"

"No. You try," he hissed.

Talon leaned over her and whispered, "Come on, Kitten. You can do this."

"Yeah, bitch, show me how tough you are," I added.

"I'm not. I'm tired, Deanna. So tired."

Talon and I looked at each other. Both of us, I knew, were wishing we could help her more through this, but we couldn't.

"You wanna lay on the bed?" I asked.

She nodded. I moved outta the way as Talon scooped her up into his arms and laid her down.

I lay next to her on the bed, and Talon knelt beside it on her other side. We both took a hand of hers each.

"You know I love you, wench, but there is no way I'm getting down the other end and lookin' at your hoo-ha."

She smiled and closed her eyes, only to open them seconds later when the contraction hit.

"Push, Kitten. Push, baby, please."

Her hand gripped ours tighter and she screamed, "I am pushing, you motherfucker." And she was; she beared down and pushed so hard, I was surprised her eyes didn't pop outta her head.

Just as I was thinkin' there was no way in fuckin' hell I

was ever going to go through this, a cry hit the room.

"We have a boy." The nurse smiled and passed him off to another nurse I hadn't seen enter the room.

"A boy! A fuckin' boy, Kitten." Talon grinned and followed the nurse who held his son. "Be careful with him. Fuck, woman, are you supposed to do that? You fuck him up, I'll hurt you."

"Talon." Zara smiled tiredly. "Let them work."

"Just take a breather, and then we'll do it all again on the next contraction," the nurse next to us said.

"Is he okay?" Zara asked.

"He's a fuckin' champ. Big and loud, baby," Talon said as he knelt back down next to his wife. He certainly was loud—the kid hadn't shut up—but then again, I'd be upset coming into a cold world after living in a warm squishy waterbed too.

"Talon," Zara cried as another pain hit.

"Kitten, baby, push again and we'll get to meet our other youngin'."

She nodded and bore down once again, ending in a scream that a smaller, quieter one replied to.

"It's a girl," the nurse said before she turned to take her over to a table.

"Kitten, fuck, I am so proud of you. So fuckin' proud,"

Talon whispered into Zara's hair. He pulled back, and that was when I saw the tears in my boo's man's eyes.

"I love you, Talon Marcus," Zara muttered.

"I love you more than my life," he said, and kissed her softly on the lips.

"Good. Now go check they aren't swapping our kids over. And quit all the cursing…they can hear you now," she ordered.

Talon laughed and replied, "I'm on it." He moved from the bed and went to check his twins.

Zara turned her head to me. "I love you too, wench."

I bit my lip and nodded as tears filled my eyes. "You saved me, Zara. I would have been lost without you. But you saved me, and I'm so happy you let me be here for this miracle. I love you too, bitch."

Griz

After the women had left, we collected the sweating men—who were now shittin' themselves—back into the front seat of the van. As Killer held a gun on them, Blue and Stoke moved the bikes to the side of the road. Travis, Warden and I climbed in the back of the van, and once we were in position with the divider open and a gun on the two up the front, Killer came around and got in with Blue and Stoke.

"I'm sure by now you can guess what the plan is," I said, "but in case you're dumb fucks and haven't—which you must be to take the women in the first place—you're taking us to Ryan's. Now start driving." The one named

Kenny started the van, did a U-turn and started off.

"How far are we from the destination?" Travis asked.

The one in the passenger seat, Nathan I think, replied, "About ten minutes."

"How many men has Ryan got at the house?" Warden asked.

"Not many, about five," Nathan said.

"You need to shut the fuck up," Kenny growled.

I hit him in the back of the head. "No, dickhead, you need to."

"You know what?" Blue started. I looked over my shoulder to see him leaning against the back of the van, but I knew once the time came, he'd be more alert and ready for the fight that was about to come. I gave him a chin lift to continue and he did. "I reckon Trav and Warden would make great brothers. We should swear them in."

I looked to Travis beside me, and then to Warden, who was holding onto the safety bar just behind Travis.

"I'm happy where I am," Warden said. "I got enough shit goin' on workin' with Vi. No offense, but being in a biker group just ain't my thing."

"None taken, but I'm sure the offer is still there, even when we tell Talon." I said. "What about you?" I asked Travis. He'd be a good asset; he's got sources in

Melbourne. It was obvious he'd do anything to protect what was his and he didn't crack under pressure.

"I'd have to talk to Violet about it," he said with an amused smile.

I chuckled, as did my brothers. We got that; Violet was another hard, ball-busting woman.

"We're nearly there," Nathan said.

"Fuckin' nark," Kenny hissed.

I hit him in the head again, making him swear.

Blue got up on his knees with his hand on the backdoors, ready to pop them open. Killer and Stoke were beside him, which left Warden, Travis and me to get out the side door.

The calm atmosphere in the van intensified into a harsher anxious one. Everyone was ready.

Duckin' my head down a bit, we pulled into a drive. Kenny went to stop there, but I ordered him to take it into the garage that was already open. Ryan's huge motherfuckin' house was in the suburbs; we couldn't risk an audience. We needed to take the fight inside.

With a hard shove on the back of Kenny's head from my gun, he finally did as I told him, and slowly drove the van into the garage. As soon as we were through, the automatic door behind us closed.

I smiled. Ryan obviously didn't want an audience either, seeing how he still thought he was kidnappin' my woman. It was pure fuckin' luck we caught them before they arrived here, because it had worked out beautifully for us.

A door in front of the van opened, and Ryan outlined the lit opening.

"What the hell are you waiting for?" he yelled.

Just as I turned to give the go-ahead to the boys up the back, dickhead Kenny screamed, "Watch out!"

It all went into chaos. My brothers jumped out the back as I knocked Kenny out with the back of my gun. Warden opened the side door, got out with his gun raised and pointed it at Ryan. He moved aside to let Travis and myself out, and I stepped up to Ryan and smiled. His eyes widened comically.

"It was the wrong move trying to take my woman, arsehole."

A shot at the front of the garage was fired. "We've got incoming," Blue called.

"They're coming in the side door, Griz," Travis said.

More shots were fired. Travis ran to the back to help out while Warden and I eyed Ryan. For some reason, he wasn't running.

He moved aside, and a few more men ran in shooting at whatever moved. I shifted back into the van, as did Warden.

"What do you want to do?" Warden asked.

"I want my hands on that motherfucker," I growled. The noise in the garage grew louder from guns, fists and voices.

"Go get him then." Warden grinned. He silently moved out of the side door of the van once again and crept to the front, where the men with guns were now standing. Warden shot and one fell; the next turned and fired on Warden, but I dove from the side of the van, fired off a shot and clipped him. Warden ran and tackled the guy to the ground as Blue came up from the other side of the garage and took down one more.

I ran for the door and went straight through. A loud clutter came from the left, so I went that way, following the wall down the hall closely, so if anything came around the corner, they wouldn't see me first before I killed them.

As I crept closer to the entry way to what looked like a living room, another loud clatter sounded, accompanied by swearing.

"Fuck, where in the hell are my keys?" Ryan cried.

I turned the corner with my gun held high and asked, "Missing something?" He was over near a black leather couch, a cushion still in his hand.

"Griz, come on. Let's just forget this. You don't owe me money any longer, and I promise I won't go after your woman."

I laughed. "Too late for that—your guy already touched her in a way I didn't like. She'll have a bruise from it for a couple of days, which means she'll remember what happened for a couple of days, and I don't like that."

"What do you want? You want money? People? I can find anyone who has done you wrong and have them gone."

"Jesus, you really are stupid. I want nothing from you; I take care of my own business. No one who has crossed me or mine has lived to see another day."

"What about Maxwell?"

"Don't worry about him; he's on my list," I glared. "Get on your knees," I snarled. He was pathetic, trying to bargain his way out of the inevitable.

He took a step back, his hand raised in front of him, and he looked down as a wet patch filled the front of his slacks. "Griz," he squeaked, "I-I'm sure we can work something out."

I shook my head at the sight in front of me. It was all the same. As soon as the shoe was on the other foot, their tough exterior faded and left a weak, useless one behind.

I scoffed, "Nothin' to work out."

"I'm sure we can figure something out." A gun was shoved into my back. I looked over my shoulder to see Kenny standing there.

Well, shit. I should have just shot the dick.

"Not today," another voice said; this time, it was behind Kenny, who in turn let out a grunted groan and fell to his knees, his gun dropping to the ground beside him.

Nathan stepped up with a knife in his hand. "He's getting away." He gestured with his chin to Ryan, who was looking frantic as he neared the front door.

I sighed, aimed and shot. Ryan fell onto his back to the wooden flooring, just out of reach of the front door.

"Because you had my back, you go. Now, before my brothers catch you," I said to Nathan as I started my way over to a moaning Ryan.

"Thanks," he said, and moved off to where, I guessed, the kitchen and backdoor was.

"Don't thank me; you haven't made it yet."

I stopped and looked down at Ryan. The fucker was actually crying as he held his stomach.

His eyes widened as I raised my gun once again and shot him in-between his eyes.

"Griz, brother, we gotta go," Blue called from the other side of the living room.

I looked up to see him with a bleeding nose and a busted-up lip. Running forward, I asked, "Everyone all right?"

With grim eyes, he shook his head.

Fuck.

Shit.

"Who?"

"Stoke. We gotta get him to a hospital. He was shot in the gut and he's bleeding out pretty bad. I think it hit something vital."

"Goddamn it," I uttered. We hit the garage just as Killer and a limping Warden were loading Stoke into the back of the van.

After Travis climbed in the driver's seat, Blue hopped in the passenger one and I ran around to the back to get in. Warden closed the door behind me. I made my way to Stoke's side; Killer was on the other, holding a folded up towel over Stoke's wound.

The garage doors opened and we took off. Both Killer and I supported Stoke, trying to keep him as still as we could as Warden watched from the backdoors of the van.

"Brother," I said, taking his hand in mine. "Dammit,

Stoke, dammit."

"S-s'all good, Grady. You know I'd do it over again if I had the chance. Always at your back, brother. Alwa—"

"Stoke. Shit, brother?"

Killer crouched over him, "He's only passed out, but his heart is slowin'."

"Fuck! Travis, drive like you did before; get us to a hospital."

Deanna

I left the happy couple to head back out the front where everyone else was waiting. Talon wanted me to announce the monsters' arrival while he helped Zara get cleaned up; they wanted to bond with the twins over breastfeeding.

Opening the doors, eight pairs of eyes were instantly latched onto me.

"We have a boy and a girl." I smiled. Clapping filled the space along with wild cheers. I searched further to see if my man was there, but he wasn't. My shoulders slumped in sadness. I would've loved to have shared this moment with him. Worry took over my body. *Was he okay? Was he hurt? Where in the fuck was he?*

I pushed it all back and slapped on my happy face. A

nurse stepped out behind me and said, "Only a few visitors for now, but they're asking for their children, Zara's parents and his sister to come in."

A tired Violet, Richard, Nancy and Cody, who took Maya's hand, walked past me as Josie and Swan came to stand in front of me. I smiled and asked, "Are you guys excited to meet…" *Crap, I didn't even know the names of the brats yet.* "…the bundles of joy?"

"Yes, very." Josie grinned behind her hand; she was often doing things like that. If she laughed, she covered her mouth, but if she forgot to at the time, she'd duck her head at the end and blush. I could only hope one day her self-esteem issues would evaporate.

"W-when?" Swan asked.

I looked over my shoulder to the doors. "I'm sure you can soon, baby. Besides, they have to announce their names." I glanced over to Julian and Mattie, who were sitting in the waiting chairs hugging. "Do you guys know what they're gonna name them?" I asked.

They looked at each other and then shook their heads.

"No," Mattie said. "It's all been very tight-lipped."

A half-hour had passed when the doors finally opened again; Violet and Zara's parents walked out with the kids, happy tears shining in their eyes.

"She wants all of you in there." Nancy smiled. "They're absolutely beautiful; I could just eat them up."

Violet walked up to me and whispered, "I'm going to catch a taxi, head home to shower and come back with Travis. I'm leaving his car here in case you need it to get Swan home."

"You're being nice again," I stated.

"I know, and believe me—I'll throw up for it later." She smiled. I smirked at her and shook my head.

I understood her need for a shower; I really wanted one too, but I'd wait. So with a thanks and a nod from me, she took off after a goodbye to everyone else.

"We're taking the kids to the cafeteria to get something to eat. Do any of you want anything?" Richard asked.

With a no from everybody, they made their way to the elevators, and Mattie, Julian, Swan, Josie and I went back into Zara's room.

She was sitting up in her bed, and even though she looked beat, she was obviously happy. I could see it in her shining eyes and the smile that played on her mouth.

I stood back with Swan, holding her hand as Julian, Mattie and Josie all gushed over the twins being held by their mum and very happy dad.

After they stepped back, I moved forward and sat Swan

on the bed beside Zara.

"Hey there, sweetie," Zara said to Swan. "Do you like the babies?"

Swan nodded, and then her head turned on its side as she asked, "Names?"

Talon cleared his throat and was about to say something, when the door to the room opened and in walked Grady. My hand went to my neck as I took him in. He was in one piece, but he had a grim look upon his face, though it quickly changed once he saw Swan and me.

Swan jumped down from the bed and ran for her father, yelling, "Daddy!"

He scooped her up in his arms and held her tightly, and then one arm came out as he eyed me. I went straight for it. I wrapped my arms around both of them, burying my head into Grady's neck.

"You okay?" I uttered.

"S'all good, darlin'. We'll talk soon."

I nodded and moved back so I could reach up and peck him on the lips.

"Will you two stop groping in front of your child? Let's hear the announcement of the names, and then we can take Swan down to the cafeteria too," Julian said.

Grady had a silent conversation with Talon through

nods and chin lifts. I would never begin to understand how that worked.

"All right," Talon started, "we've been going over some names for a while, but we've finally decided, and even if you hate them, we won't give a fuck. For our son," he lifted his arms cradling the sleeping boy, "it's Drake." His eyes held mine as stupid, ugly tears filled my own eyes. Holy shit, why would they do that?

"Hun, we wanted to pass on the Drake name in some form. I knew how much they meant to you and how much you mean to me. From what you've told us, they were amazing people who deserved to have their name preserved, so that's why we chose it."

I could only nod. If I opened my mouth, I was likely to cry.

"And for our beautiful girl, her name is Ruby," Talon said and smiled. "Maya and Cody helped with that one. We were sure damned surprised that they actually kept it to themselves." He chuckled.

"They're really nice," Josie commented.

"They're great," Mattie said.

"I love them!" Julian clapped. "Right, now come on, sweet pea," he said to Swan and took her from Grady's arms. "Let's go get some food."

Mattie gently grabbed Josie's hand, who I saw flinch, but he ignored it and started for the door. "We'll be back soon," he said, and then left with the rest.

As soon as the door closed, Talon growled, "Now, you wanna tell us what in the fuck is going on?"

"It's been handled, so you don't need to worry about it right now."

"I don't give a shit if it's handled. Explain, brother."

I stepped out of Grady's arms and went over to sit on the edge of the bed. Grady came up behind me and rested his hands on my shoulders, and I leaned back into him to absorb his warmth.

"Violet was at my house—"

Zara gasped. "Is she still alive?"

With an eye roll, I said, "Very funny, wench, and yes, you just saw she was. She came to tell me Jason got released early."

"You didn't tell me this," Grady snapped.

"Well, I didn't actually have time now, did I?"

"Griz," Talon said. I lifted my head to see yet another fuckin' silent conversation was going on. I was sure this one said in their caveman ways, *She'll need more protection,* with a response of, *I'm on it. Ugg, ugg, grunt, fart and groan.*

"Anyway," I said, "we went into the house, and two men were there waiting and took us." Zara gasped once again. "It's all good, as you can see. Violet had a tracking device; the guys found us and we came here."

"Then who put that fuckin' bruise and bump on your head?" Talon asked.

Grady grunted, "One of the guys."

"Where is he now? And who in the hell would take Hawks' property?"

"He's dead. It was Ryan's smart idea to try and get money out of me."

"Tell me he failed," Zara asked. Holy shit. Did she mean what I thought she meant?

Grady nodded. "He's also dead."

"Good," she said, and then glanced at me. "Oh, don't look so shocked. Being around him," she gestured to Talon, "for so long, I learn what's good for our family and what's not. I don't like most of it, but if it's to protect what's ours, then it has to be done."

"I agree," I said, and I did.

"There was one problem though; Stoke's being operated on as we speak."

"Fuck. What happened?" Talon asked.

"Bullet to the stomach. It must have hit something

vital."

"The bastard better pull through," Talon uttered.

"I'm sure he will," Zara said and placed her hand on Talon's, which was holding Drake's. He met her worried gaze and nodded.

"We better head off, brother," Grady said. "I'm sure you're both tired."

"Pfft. He's not the one who gave birth to two watermelons. Both kids had huge heads…must have their father's ego." She always liked to lighten the mood and it worked.

Talon grinned at his wife, and then turned to Grady and me. "Thanks for coming, Griz. And you too, Hell Mouth."

"Always a pleasure when I'm around." I grinned and then sobered. "We'll keep you updated with Stoke." I looked to Grady for confirmation and he nodded.

We said our final goodbyes and then made our way to the cafeteria.

Griz

Nancy saw how exhausted both Deanna and I were—
mentally and physically—so she offered to mind Swan for
the night, and Swan was more than happy to go with her.

I had Pick drive us home in Travis's car; everyone else
wanted to stay a little longer, so Pick was gonna head back
after dropping Dee and me home.

Even though it felt fuckin' weird, I got in the back with
Deanna and brought her close to me, leaving Pick up front
alone like some damned driver of the rich and famous.

"Have you heard any more about Stoke?" Pick asked.

"Nah, not yet. I'm sure Killer will ring as soon as he
knows."

"Do you want to head back there? After Pick drops us off, we can take my car," Deanna offered.

"Darlin', it's so fuckin' sweet of you to ask, but not tonight. Ask me again in the mornin'." What I wanted and needed the most was to lay down between the sheets and in-between my woman's legs. I needed to feel she was there, safe and in our house.

It made me feel like an arse about Stoke, but I was sure he would've done the same. There was nothing I could do for him at the hospital. If and when we heard the outcome, we would deal then. We would take care of him one way or another. If I knew how to fuckin' operate on a body, there would be no way I'd be in the back of this car, but I didn't, so like I said, there was nothing I could do for Stoke right then.

The car pulled to a slow stop out the front of our house. I gave a chin lift and thanked Pick as we got out, and with dragging feet, we made our way up the walk.

"Griz?" Pick called.

"Be back in a sec, princess," I sighed to Deanna. She smiled, gave me a quick kiss and moved off to the front door.

I turned around and was walking back to the car, when I saw something shining in the living room window—

something that shouldn't have been there, something I had never seen before.

Ignoring Pick, I started to make my way back to Deanna just as she was unlocking the door. She opened it and took a step inside. I watched as her body startled. She looked back outside to me with tears in her eyes, shook her head and closed the door in my face.

Fuck, fuck, fuck.

He was in there.

Jason Drake was in the house with my woman.

Alone.

No matter how much I wanted to bust down the door, I didn't. I couldn't, because there was no telling what kind of situation Deanna was in.

I stepped back and the curtain twitched. He was watching, waiting for me to make a move. Did he know I was aware he was in there? I wasn't sure.

"Fine, bitch, be that way," I yelled.

Christ, I hoped to hell he bought this shit acting.

"I'll be back in the morning for my stuff," I called. It damn near burned me inside to turn back around and walk back down the path to the still-waiting car I climbed into.

"Trouble?" Pick asked.

"He's in there," I hissed. "Drive around the corner and

park. We're going in through the back yard on foot."

"Who's in there, Griz?" he asked.

"Her foster brother, the man who killed his own parents and is about to harm my woman. Fuck!" I yelled.

"We need back-up?" he asked as he put the car in park and I jumped out.

Pick was around the car in seconds and I replied, "No. Too late. We're doin' this...unless you don't want to?"

"I'm there, brother." He nodded.

"Right. Let's kick it."

Adrenaline pumped through me. Even though I was dead on my feet, the need to save my woman overran my body and pushed any other feelings or thoughts out. Pick and I jumped over four backyard fences and finally reached the small, familiar yard that belonged to Dee. The back deck was dark, as was the house, except for one light in the living room. I was used to the house, so I knew what I was looking at coming from the kitchen window—the lamp that sat next to the couch in the front room was on.

I signalled for Pick to keep his eyes and ears open; he gave a swift nod and went around the side of the house. I crept to the back door with my keys in my hand. My grip was on the handle when I heard a scream.

Deanna

Ten Minutes Earlier

Unlocking the front door, I was more than ready for bed; I was ready for my man to take me slow and deep to release some of the stress that had built up as I waited for him to arrive at the hospital.

I stepped through and turned halfway so I was facing the living room. My eyes hit him straight away. Jason was standing near the window smirking at me.

My heart hit my feet.

Shattered. That was how I felt. Tears filled my eyes, because I knew this was the moment I was probably going to die, or try my fuckin' hardest not to.

I had people to live for; I just hoped that'd make me strong enough to get through…without bringing anyone else down in the process.

I glanced back outside to see Grady making his way back up the footpath, a stern, worried look held within his eyes. I shook my head and closed the front door in his face, quickly locking it.

"Fine, bitch, be that way," Griz's booming voice rang through the room. "I'll be back in the morning for my stuff."

Jason raised an eyebrow at me. "Smart move, Deanna," he said.

He looked the same as he had eight years ago, with the same dark red hair and light green crazy eyes. He was still tall and thin, but I could tell he must have been working out while in jail. His muscles were more defined now.

Fuck. Did that mean he was stronger?

"I don't have the money, Jason."

"Don't bullshit me. I know you've tried to spend it, but the amount they would have left you could not be spent in one lifetime. Though, that's not all I want Deanna. You should know this."

I nodded. He wanted my life.

"I just can't understand why you would be so stupid to move to a holiday house *my* parents owned. You made this so easy for me."

"I know."

He studied me where I stood behind the couch.

"Why don't you seem…scared?"

I pretended to think about it. "Honestly, I'm not sure.

Maybe it has something to do with the thought it won't be *my* life ending tonight."

Shit, fuck, shit. Please buy the crap I spew.

He laughed and took a step forward. "I highly doubt that. You see, I learned many things while I was in prison."

"I'm sure you did. A time well fuckin' spent for the crime you committed, eh?"

"Oh, you still haven't broken out of that habit. It's ugly, Deanna; you need to control your language." He casually reached over to the chair next to him and ran a finger along it as he smiled. "But then again, I won't have to put up with it much longer."

"Hmm, probably not, because you'll be dead."

He chuckled. "Are you really going to try, Deanna? Or is it that you're stalling? Do you think the man you arrived with will come back and save you? Is that it?"

My eyes widened. He had better damn well not be. I'd have to hurt Grady if he tried anything. This was my fight.

"No," I said, "you heard him."

He crossed his arms over his chest. "Even if he was, it wouldn't bother me. It would just be another person to kill, and I've missed that, Deanna. I've missed slicing my knife through flesh and bone, and the way my victims would cry or hiss their pain. I would love to see what that man would

271

do."

"You won't get the chance, Jason," I growled.

"Maybe, we will see."

"You're a sick bastard, you know that? Sick," I yelled, only to jump to the side to miss the knife that whizzed past my head and embed itself into the wall near the hallway to the stairs. With a thump, I landed on the ground with my head just past the couch. I glanced from the knife back up to see Jason grinning.

"Tut-tut, Deanna—language."

"Fuck you," I yelled, and then screamed when another knife was thrown my way. I ducked down and reached under the couch to where the gun I had strapped to the bottom of it waited. I pulled it free and stood.

"You need to stop, J-Jason," I said, and then damned my voice when it shook.

"Deanna, oh dear, sweet Deanna, you see, I don't think I do. You won't pull the trigger."

"I will. I fuckin' will," I yelled and brought my other hand up to help the one holding the gun, because it was shaking like shit.

Stupid, cocksucking nerves.

I can do this. I need to do this. It will bring me peace. It has to.

"Deanna?" I looked out the corner of my eye to see Grady with a gun held high, and just like mine, it was pointed directly at Jason.

"What are you doing here?" I hissed through clenched teeth. "Th-this isn't your fight; it's mine."

"No, darlin', it ain't just yours. It's ours. If you want justice for what he's done, *we* will bring it."

Oh, fuck. Shit.

Tears filled my eyes.

"Grady," I sighed.

"Isn't this sweet?" Jason cooed. His eyes landed on Griz. "Move another step toward her and she dies." He pulled a knife from the back of his pants, and with it in his hand, he aimed it at me. "I'm great at hitting my target." He smiled.

"You fuckin' hurt her, I will—"

"What...kill me? I've been dead ever since she came into my life. If I die here tonight, at least I know I'll be taking her with me," he sneered.

"No, you won't," Grady growled. His gaze came to me; I could feel the heat of it on me. "Dee, walk slowly over to me."

"No," I uttered, "I-I have to do this." The damned gun in my hands was shaking so badly, I didn't know if I'd actually hit anything.

"Deanna," Grady said, his tone holding that familiar warning.

"This is great and all, but I'm bored," Jason sighed. He flung the knife just as a boom echoed in the house and a loud crash of glass breaking filled the room, all of it happening in seconds.

I went crashing to the floor when a large form tackled me.

Dazed and confused, I looked up at Grady where he stood above me. If he was there, then who in the fuck was on me?

Blinking, I turned my head to see Pick staring back.

"You all right, Hell Mouth?" he asked. I nodded.

"No time for sleepin', you two. We gotta do a quick clean-up. I'm sure one of your neighbours has called the cops by now, darlin'," Grady said and reached a hand down, and as Pick got off me, I placed my hand in it and he pulled me up to stand.

I looked over to Jason, wondering why he wasn't saying anything, only to find my answer.

"Dammit, Grady, you killed him," I snapped and stomped my foot.

He chuckled, grabbed me and wrapped his arms around

me. "There was no way that fucker was going to wreck what we've got."

I gave him an eye roll. "Well, I know that, but you could have let me do it."

"Next time, darlin'. You were just lucky that knife didn't plant in your head." He gestured with his chin. I looked over my shoulder to see a knife in the wall behind where I had been standing.

Fuck me. I could have died if they hadn't been there.

"Thank you," I muttered and glanced to Pick, who was now wrapping a dead Jason up in some plastic. Where he got it from, I didn't know, and I didn't care. "Both of you, thanks."

"It's what families do for each other," Pick said.

"Ain't that right." Grady smiled. I grinned back up at him.

"I love you," I said.

His eyes transformed in front of me; they became hooded and heated. His smile widened into a shit-eatin' grin.

"We choose some funny moments to tell each other."

I laughed. "I know, but I love it—this, you and every moment we have, no matter the situation—as long as we're together."

"Fuck yeah." He gave my body a squeeze. "As long as we're together."

"Now get your sweet arse to helping Pick. I hear some sirens on the way," I told him with a wink.

"Bossy, bitch."

Grinning, I said, "And you love it."

Epilogue

Deanna

One Month Later

Excitement and nerves swirled through my body. I felt all girly and shit, wanting to squeal, clap or jump up and down. My man was on his way home, and I had a surprise for him. Two, actually. One, I wasn't sure how he'd react to...okay, I wasn't sure how he'd react to either of the surprises, which was why I was so fuckin' nervous as well.

Everything had settled down after that night, after the cops left believing our story. We told them Grady had been drunk—which he acted out fuckin' superbly—and had fallen through the window, and once they saw he was no threat to me, they left. Pick ended up bringing around

Travis's car. They loaded up Jason, and as far as I knew, they found a special place to get rid of the body—a place I was told no one would find. I didn't want to know where exactly, because I didn't care.

I was free.

It was as if a weight had been lifted from me. No, it would never help the grief I still felt for the loss of the Drakes, but it did ease it enough I knew my life would now be lighter.

Also that night, Grady had gotten a call waking us in the middle of night; it had been Killer. Stoke had pulled through his operation and was on his way to mending. Things couldn't be better—well, unless Grady liked his surprises, then things could get even better.

I heard the front door open from where I stood in the kitchen.

"What in the goddamn hell is that?" Grady yelled.

I grinned. He'd found my first surprise.

Heavy footstep pounded and I looked to the doorway. He came in wearing his usual jeans, tee and biker vest over the top. He started straight for me.

"Deanna Drake, what is that fuckin' *thing* in the living room in a playpen?"

I backed up. He stopped at one end of the kitchen

bench, and I was at the other end smiling like a fool.

"That, babe, would be your surprise."

A tiny yip came from the living room.

"What is it?" he growled. "No, don't fuckin' tell me. It ain't staying. It's damn ugly, woman, and I don't want Swan gettin' attached to something that isn't staying around."

With my hands on my hips, I glared. "It fuckin' is staying, arsehole. Swan is going to love it, just like I do, and I know you will...eventually."

"No, I won't," he yelled, and then calmed enough to ask, "Where is Swan?"

"She's at Zara's. Drake and Ruby love her. We'll go get her soon. Plus, I told them I wanted to surprise you with Oscar."

"What's Oscar? That *thing*?"

"He is not a thing. He's a Pomeranian and cute as a button."

"Fuck. Do you hear yourself? *Cute as a button?* My woman doesn't say that shit. He's changing you already."

"Well, it's time I did, and besides, I got him for a good reason."

"What? To use as a fuckin' mop? It's that damned fluffy enough."

I giggled. "No, smartarse, I thought..."

"What, darlin'?" he prompted when I paused.

"I…he, um. I thought…that, well…he'd be good practice. I mean, he's a puppy, and he'll have needs and shit, so I thought we could have a bit of practice for when the time came when we'd… um, maybe have a baby."

Holy shit. That was harder than I thought it would be.

I glanced up to see Grady's eyes were wide.

Maybe it wasn't a good surprise after all. Goddamn it, I shouldn't have gone off the pill. I only missed that morning's, so I could do a catch up. We'd just have to not have sex for twenty-four hours…or some shit like that.

I jumped when I felt a hand caress my face. With his fingers under my chin, Grady turned my head to look up at him.

He seemed calm now. "You mean, you want to have a kid with me?"

"Um...yes?"

He grinned so wide his molars were showing. "First things first," he said, and I raised my eyebrow at him.

He got down on one knee.

My heart wanted out. I was sure it would have crawled outta my mouth if I wasn't clenching my teeth together so hard. Tears filled my eyes. Was this really happening?

"Deanna Drake, the moment you came into my life, it

changed. I love how you fight back. I love that you don't take shit and that you know when to be sweet, sexy, mean and bitchy. But most of all, I love *you*, every fuckin' way you are—and yeah, even when you're moody. I want to know if you'd be willing to put up with me and the way I am. Will you marry me?"

"Damn you for making me cry, but it's a yes. Hell yes, I'm more than willing to put up with you and your demanding ways." I smiled. His eyes softened as he pulled out a gold ring with a beautiful princess-cut diamond out of his club-vest and slid it on my finger.

As he stood, my tee came up and off, and thrown to the side. He kissed me hard, sweet and long.

Coming up for breath, I asked, "W-what are we doing? We have to go get Swan and introduce her to Oscar."

"Later, I'll let those two meet, but right now, we gotta get down to business," he said and kissed my shoulder. His hands reached around to unclasp my bra. He pulled it from my shoulders, threw it to where my tee was on the floor and then palmed my breasts.

"What business?"

"Making a baby. I want this to happen as soon as fuckin' possible. I cannot wait to fill you with my seed and for it to stay there to make a miracle."

Well, hell. When he said it like that, how could I resist?

I ripped his tee over his head and dropped it to the floor. My hands went to his jeans. Popping the button, I slid down the fly and gripped his hard cock tucked inside, making him hiss.

My jean shorts were undone and pushed down my legs with my underwear.

"Spread 'em," Grady growled. I did; I moved my feet apart enough he could run a finger over my folds. With ease—because I was so fuckin' turned on and wet—his finger slipped inside, and then pulled out to rub against my clit.

"Shit," I uttered. My head fell forward to his chest as I gripped his dick harder and ran my hand up and down his length.

"Step outta your pants, darlin'," he ordered.

After I did just that, he wrapped a hand around each of my thighs and picked me up to sit on the kitchen bench, my hand falling free of his boxers—not that it bothered me, because I knew what was coming next. I watched as he rid himself of the rest of his clothes.

He stood back, his cock at full attention and his eyes on me. He licked his lips and then grinned. "Put your feet up on the edge of the bench, knees wide for me."

"Grady," I warned. I didn't want to play games; I wanted him now.

"Deanna, do it." He glared.

With an eye roll, I brought my legs up and parted them far apart so the most intimate part of me was on display.

"Beautiful," he hissed. "Fuck, please play with yourself," he asked and wrapped his large palm around his dick and started to stroke it.

I ran my hand over my breast, down my belly and outlined my folds with a finger. His heated, hungry eyes ate it all up.

Dipping one finger into my hole, my head fell back and I moaned, only it turned into a gasp when my hand was pushed to the side and Grady's mouth was on my pussy, licking and tonguing me all over.

"Jesus. Fuck, that feels good, Grady," I hissed when he gripped my hips tightly and drove his tongue straight into me over and over.

"Oh, hell. I'm gonna—"

"Not yet," he growled. He stood with his cock in his hand and stepped forward. He lined his dick up and slowly entered me, and his thumb slid over my clit. There was no way I could have held off. My walls gripped him tighter as I came around his entering dick.

"Darlin', Christ," he snarled. He reached for me, and with a hand on each arm, he pulled me up. I wrapped my arms around his neck as his folded around my waist. Our lips met and as we kissed; the taste of myself on his mouth was something erotic. Grady slid back and forth in an agonizingly slow motion, and I loved every fuckin' second of it.

His lips left mine, and I met his warm gaze. "Are you ready?"

"Yes."

"Fuck, woman, I'm gonna come any second. We're about to make something special."

I gripped his arse and smiled. "May not happen the first time."

"Fuck that," he growled. "It will with my swimmers." He grinned. "Christ," he hissed as he moved his hand from my hip to in-between our bodies, and with one flick on my clit, a moan left my lips as I came once again. With a grunt and then a groan, Grady pumped his seed into me.

He pulled back and looked at me. I knew I was smiling like a fool; I liked the thought of having him inside of me. Even though we'd done it many times, this time was exceptional.

It was something else.

It was us.

"We're in this together," Grady said.

"Together." I nodded and reached my hand up to touch his cheek. "I can't wait."

"Me neither. Even if you do drive me nuts, it'll all be worth it." He smiled. I gave him a light slap on his cheek. His eyes widened. "You wanna play rough? Give me a minute and we'll play it my way."

I laughed. "We can't. We have to get Swan."

"Bullshit. She won't mind waiting," he said as he slowly slid his cock out of me.

"We have to check on the dog."

"He can wait," he said with a hard thrust back inside. "We're busy."

"Grady," I snapped and then rolled my eyes. I knew there was no way he would listen. I felt his dick harden even more within me.

I guess Swan and the dog could wait just a little bit longer.

The End

BLUE AND CLARINDA'S STORY COMING SOON.

Made in the USA
San Bernardino, CA
16 February 2016